OTHER YEARLING BOOKS YOU WILL ENJOY

FAST FORWARD: A DANGEROUS SECRET
Ian Bone

CHIG AND THE SECOND SPREAD
Gwenyth Swain

THE GYPSY GAME
Zilpha Keatley Snyder

WITH LOVE FROM SPAIN, MELANIE MARTIN
Carol Weston

BLUBBER
Judy Blume

BOYS AGAINST GIRLS
Phyllis Reynolds Naylor

MOLLY MCGINTY HAS A REALLY GOOD DAY
Gary Paulsen

THE UNSEEN

Zilpha Keatley Snyder

A Yearling Book

Published by Yearling, an imprint of Random House Children's Books
a division of Random House, Inc., New York

Visit us on the Web! www.randomhouse.com/kids

Educators and librarians, for a variety of teaching tools, visit us at
www.randomhouse.com/teachers

ISBN: 0-440-41930-1

Reprinted by arrangement with Delacorte Press

Printed in the United States of America

August 2005

10 9 8 7 6 5 4

TO TWO WONDERFUL EDITORS WHOSE DEDICATION,
INTEGRITY AND ARTISTRY MADE ALL THE DIFFERENCE

TO KAREN WOJTYLA

AND IN MEMORIAM
TO JEAN KARL

FOREWORD

THIS STORY REALLY began many years ago when, as a freshman in college, I heard a professor say that *it might be possible that we are all constantly surrounded by entities and events of which we are completely unaware because of the limitations of our sense organs.* Of course I knew that there are limits to our ability to see, hear, smell, taste and touch. For example—our human noses can't begin to experience a dog's complicated world of aromas. But it had never before occurred to me to wonder what other unheard, unsmelled, untasted, untouched and unseen entities might exist all around us.

I don't remember anything else the professor had to say that day. At that point I must have gone into a trance, enchanted by the possibilities. A trance that has recurred now and then over the years, during which I often asked myself, "What might be out there, all around me? What would it look like if I could see it? In what way might it interact with me?" As I imagined answers to those questions, I also began to consider ways I might write about the fascinating images the professor's suggestion brought to mind. Here are some of those images—as creatures of *The Unseen.*

Zilpha Keatley Snyder

1

IT ALL BEGAN on a cold day in early autumn when a girl named Alexandra Hobson was playing a dangerous game in a forbidden forest. The game, about an enchanted creature, half human and half animal, had been inspired by the fact that Alexandra, or Xandra, as she preferred to be called, believed herself to be enchanted in some deeply secret and very private way. In a way that ordinary human beings could never understand or appreciate. Particularly not the humans who happened to be members of her own family and who, in spite of what most people thought, were all hopelessly ordinary.

As for the forbidden forest? The forest was real enough, acres and acres of undeveloped timberland that started right behind the Hobsons' property and stretched out toward the mountains. And the forbidden part was real too. Forbidden by people who insisted that a forest wasn't a safe place for a twelve-year-old girl to spend so much time, at least not all by herself.

And so it happened that on that particular cloudy afternoon nobody knew where Xandra was or what she was doing. Not that any of her siblings would have cared to know, except so that they could tell and cause trouble. In the Hobson household causing trouble for Xandra had always been a favorite pastime.

She hadn't meant to go very far that day, but she'd gotten caught up in the game about being an enchanted woodland creature, and one thing and one forest pathway led to another. She'd skirted the edge of the marsh, crossed Cascade Creek by jumping from one rock to another, and kept going on, deeper into the forest.

This time the game concerned a unicorn, a magical creature that could be seen only by royal princesses or enchanted people. She was closing in on the unicorn, imagining fleeting glimpses of its slender legs and glowing golden horn, when she suddenly arrived at a place she had never been before. She had come out of dense forest into a small circular clearing carpeted with a thick layer of vines and ferns and surrounded by tall overhanging trees. She was turning in a circle, admiring the peaceful beauty of the small meadowlike area, when she was startled by a sudden sound.

She'd heard what? Gunfire? Yes. Definitely gunfire. Two shots in rapid succession. Frozen by surprise, Xandra was standing motionless when she became aware of a snapping, crackling sound in the branches over her head. She jumped back, throwing up her arms to protect her face, and when she took them down, there it was, only a few feet away.

Lying on a mound in the center of the vine-covered clearing, very close to Xandra's feet, was a large white bird. As she stared in shocked surprise, it fluttered weakly and then lay still. At first she was too horrified and angry to be frightened or even to remember why she ought to be, completely blocking out all the times she'd been warned about what might happen to her if she went into the woods alone, particularly during hunting season.

It was a big bird, its body larger than a pigeon's, but completely, purely white. Its wings, fanned out on the gray earth, gleamed like sunlit snow—except where an ugly smear of red ran along the edge of the right wing and trickled down onto the grass. Muttering, "How could they? How could anyone shoot something so beautiful?" Xandra dropped to her knees, but as she stretched out her arms the bird began to move. Lifting a sleek, tear-shaped head, it opened its long golden beak and gave a mournful cry. "Oh," Xandra gasped, "you're alive."

The wounded bird raised its head on its long curved neck and looked at her. Looked long and carefully, turning slowly to examine her with one glittering, jewel-like eye and then the other. Then it crooned again and began to try to pull its long slender legs under its body. It was still struggling to get to its feet when Xandra became aware of a series of terrifying sounds: shouting voices, crashing underbrush, and then trampling feet and the barking of a dog.

They were coming. The hunters were coming to get their prey. To crush it into a bag full of dead game, or to hang it from someone's belt by its long delicate legs.

Scooping the white bird up into her arms, Xandra turned and ran.

At first she ran directly toward home, but then, remembering something she'd read about how to escape bloodhounds, she headed for the creek. She stopped only for a moment at the rocky bank, then jumped out into the water and began to wade, working her way upstream.

The streambed was paved with slippery, moss-covered rocks, and the cold water quickly saturated her shoes. The depth of the water varied as she moved forward. Sometimes it was only a few inches deep, but now and again it flowed well above her knees, soaking the hem of her skirt. The howling of the hound grew louder and as she slipped and stumbled forward, she wondered frantically if it was really true that a hunting hound would lose the scent if its prey ran through flowing water. Or was she freezing her legs and ruining her new shoes for nothing?

The dog's howls grew louder and closer, and now Xandra could hear the voices of the hunters—hoarse, threatening voices, calling to each other and to the hound. Shaking, almost choking with fear, she stumbled on, slipping and sliding, now and then falling to her knees. With the motionless bird still cradled in both of her arms, she had to struggle clumsily to get back onto her feet. She was cold and soggy, her knees were skinned and bruised and her plaid skirt was wet almost to her waist before she became aware that the sounds of pursuit had begun to fade. The howls and shouts were growing dimmer and farther away. But even after she was fairly sure she had succeeded in throwing the hounds off the trail, she stumbled on. And all the while the bird continued to lie warm and dry in her cradling arms. Still alive? she began to wonder. Or had the poor thing died of its wounds, or perhaps of sheer fright?

The howls and shouts were long gone before Xandra dared to slow her pace, leave the streambed and scramble up the shallow bank. In her arms, the bird lay absolutely still. Putting it gently down on a patch of grass, she was looking for a solemn and secret place to leave its poor dead body when it raised its head, and once again she heard the soft, sobbing call.

It was much later when a damp and bedraggled Xandra Hobson, still carrying the wounded but now definitely living bird, pushed open the heavy back gate of 75 Heritage Avenue, closed it firmly behind her and realized that, for once, she was glad to be there.

Extremely glad, in spite of the fact that there had been times when she'd imagined, even pretended, that she lived somewhere else. Times in fact when she'd actually denied living at the expensive end of Heritage Avenue in the house that one of her smart-mouthed siblings had nicknamed the Hobson Habitat. She wasn't sure why she avoided being identified as a Hobson, except that she knew from past experience that once people knew who she was, she would have to listen to them rave about all her gorgeous and talented brothers and sisters. (Or *siblings,* as Xandra preferred to call them. There was something warm and cozy sounding about "brothers and sisters" that had very little to do with the way Xandra felt about her fellow Hobsons.)

But on that particular afternoon, with the hunters and their ferocious dog somewhere close behind her, the solid stone walls of the Hobson Habitat were a welcome sight. After a quick glance around to make sure she was not going to be seen, either by a sibling or by Otto, the Hobsons' gardener, Xandra made her way across the lawn and around several carefully landscaped flower beds on her way to the basement door.

The huge basement of the Hobson Habitat was as hopelessly dusty and cluttered as the rest of the house was sleek and shiny. Over the years it had become the dumping place for all sorts of furniture and equipment that no one used anymore but might want again at some future time. Starting just inside the door and spreading out in every direction were dozens of boxes and trunks and barrels and filing cabinets. And in between everything else there were objects too big for containers. All sorts of Hobson artifacts, such as teetering stacks of skateboards, skis, scooters, golf carts, hockey sticks, tennis rackets and the scattered remains of an elaborate model railroad. And here and there among the toys and sports equipment, many different kinds of housecleaning equipment, such as rug shampooers, floor waxers and vacuum cleaners. None of which—none of the sports stuff and certainly none of the cleaning gadgets—interested Xandra in the slightest.

But farther on, way back behind the furnace, if you knew how to find it, there was an entirely different scene. Getting there wasn't easy. The furnace itself was an enormous black box, out of which great fat heat vents snaked off toward every part of the house. It was necessary to wind your way between boxes and barrels and stacks of stuff and then duck under a couple of sagging heat vents before you came to a place that no one in the family ever visited—no one except Xandra. A place that had been, for a long time, a very private and secret hideout for her special friends who happened to be animals. And where now, as always, she immediately felt better. Safer, calmer and more at home.

It was in that small space behind the furnace that Xandra had fed and cared for a variety of infant or ailing creatures, but only until they were strong enough to make it on their own or could be adopted by families who, unlike the Hobson parents, weren't allergic to or afraid of pets of any kind.

Against one wall were the cages and boxes where various animals had lived and where, by the light of two narrow windows high up on the wall, Xandra had fed and cared for them. Creatures that had lived behind the furnace at least temporarily included any number of baby birds, two litters of abandoned kittens, an orphaned baby skunk, a slightly chewed-up garden snake she'd rescued from a neighbor's bulldog and a half-grown barn owl whose larger siblings had pushed it out of the nest. Ratchet, the noisy barn owl baby, had been one of Xandra's favorites. Having had so much personal experience with pushy siblings, she couldn't help feeling a special sympathy for the evicted owl.

So now, safe at last in the dark, smelly privacy of her secret hideout, she settled the white bird into a large carton padded with straw and equipped with a bowl of water. Although it shrank away from the touch of her hand, it seemed quite calm when she reached in to put the water bowl in place, only turning its head from side to side to watch what she was doing.

It seemed much stronger now, its head held high on its long slender neck. The blood she had seen on its right wing seemed to have disappeared. By the time she was ready to leave, the bird was sitting up with its snowy wings tucked in and its long legs folded neatly beneath its body. On her way out, preparing to duck under the first furnace vent, Xandra looked back and caught her breath in surprise. Even in the dimly lit basement, the bird's feathers glistened so brightly that it seemed to be surrounded by a mysterious halo of light. "Goodbye, you beautiful thing," she whispered. "I'll be back as soon as I find out what you are and what you like to eat."

Inside the house she stopped long enough to take off her soggy shoes before she made her way quietly up the back stairs and down the hall to her own room. A room where two whole walls were covered by bookshelves, and where, among dozens of books about birds and animals, she quickly located an illustrated volume on local birds. It didn't take long to find out what she needed to know. The bird was probably an egret or something very similar, and it would need to eat things like frogs and insects and small fish. She knew where she could find such things, of course, at a place where Cascade Creek flowed out into a series of quiet, shallow ponds, but that would have to wait until tomorrow. There wasn't time to get to the ponds and back before dinner. But in the meantime . . .

In the meantime, it suddenly occurred to her, there was the aquarium. The enormous aquarium, practically an indoor lake, full of all kinds of exotic and expensive tropical fish, which belonged to Quincy, the oldest, biggest and possibly most hateful of the siblings. Only a moment later, standing in the doorway of the fish collector's room, Xandra was peering across what closely resembled a full-fledged scientific laboratory and plotting her raid on the aquarium. She worked her way around science fair displays decorated with blue ribbons, and desks and tables covered with microscopes and racks of test tubes—plus, and this was particularly annoying, Quincy's very own television.

Not that having a television in your own room was unusual on Heritage Avenue, where most kids did. Most kids, but not the ones at the Hobson Habitat, where there was a strict rule against it until you were eighteen years old. Giving the shiny new TV a resentful glance, Xandra moved carefully and quickly across the room, knowing that the eighteen-year-old owner of the TV—not to mention his own car—might arrive home at any time. But then, peering into the watery depths of the aquarium, with the fishnet already in her hand, she changed her mind.

Why did she change her mind about kidnapping a fat and juicy zebra fish or perhaps the beautiful, brightly colored angelfish? At first she wasn't too sure. It was definitely not that she was terrified about what the aquarium-owning sibling would do to her if he learned who had taken his precious fish. That was a risk she was willing to take. After all, she didn't plan to confess and he would have no proof. But there were other reasons. The main one seemed to be that the fish were beautiful creatures too, and after all, they really couldn't help being owned by someone as mean as a Hobson teenager. And also, there was the probability that a spicy tropical fish might not be good for the digestive system of a purely white, nontropical bird—

particularly one that was already in a weakened condition. And besides, Xandra suddenly realized, there might be an easier solution. A brine shrimp solution.

Cluttering up a family refrigerator with jars of smelly brine shrimp to feed his fancy fish had been one of the aquarium owner's more annoying habits. But at that particular moment, a habit that suddenly met with Xandra's approval. Checking her watch, Xandra decided there was just about time to change into dry clothing, make a quick and stealthy stop at a particular refrigerator, visit the basement and arrive at the dinner table only a little bit later than usual.

Again, the beautiful bird considered her calmly as she put the cup into its box. It was almost as if it knew she was trying to help. It really did know, she decided as it turned its head on its long graceful neck to look down at the brine shrimp with apparent interest and then up again at Xandra. She was even more certain that the bird knew far too much to be an ordinary marsh-dwelling member of the heron family. As she prepared to leave the basement, Xandra stopped long enough to tell it so.

"I know you're not just an ordinary egret," she told the bird. "I know that you're an enchanted creature. And I'm pretty sure that you were there in my forest for some important reason."

The bird listened, turning its tear-shaped head and nodding as if agreeing with what she had to say. She felt sure it was agreeing. And later that night, sitting on the window seat in her room, she stared down into the dark garden and told herself she would soon find out what that reason could be. Why the enchanted bird had been in her forest and just how she was to be rewarded for rescuing it.

But the next morning when she made a quick stop in the basement on her way to catch the bus, the carton held only the grassy nest, the water bowl and an empty cup. The bird was gone. All that remained was one long, softly quivering white feather. But from that moment, from that breath-catching, heart-racing moment when she first saw the beautiful feather, Xandra guessed the truth. The feather was a magical gift, given to her as a promise that she would be rewarded for rescuing an enchanted creature. And she must find a way to keep it with her wherever she went.

2

XANDRA HAD NO intention of telling anyone about the mysterious bird and its magical feather. Especially not Belinda. In fact she had never before had the slightest inclination to tell the girl named Belinda anything at all. And afterward she found it difficult to remember just how it had happened.

One reason that telling Belinda was incredibly unlikely was that she and Xandra had never before talked to each other about anything. Not even once. And another reason was that Belinda was probably the weirdest person in Mr. Fernandez's seventh-grade language arts class.

There was, for instance, her general appearance. Belinda's long dark hair hung down her back in ugly, unwashed strands, and in cold weather she often wore the jacket of a man's business suit over her dingy and obviously secondhand school uniform. The ratty old suit jacket that seemed to be her cold-weather coat had a dangling fringe of ragged lining and was so much too big for her that the long sleeves had to be rolled up into fat doughnuts to allow the tips of her fingers to be seen. The gossip was that she was a Scholie, a scholarship student, one of the few kids who were allowed to attend Carter Academy even though their parents couldn't afford to pay the fees.

She acted weird too. Most of the time she was completely silent, not trying to talk to anyone, but sometimes she suddenly had a lot to say in class about things no one else knew or cared about. Things like ancient civilizations and extinct animals.

There had been times, when Belinda had first joined the class, that Xandra had been tempted to stand up for the new girl, to yell at her tormentors and let them know what she thought of people who picked on helpless things. She'd even started to yell once when a mean little fifth grader was jumping around Belinda on the playground calling her stupid names. But she'd changed her mind when she'd noticed that some of the girls who called themselves Marcie's Mob were watching. When she'd noticed that the Mob girls seemed to think the fifth grader was pretty amusing, Xandra had shut her mouth and kept it shut.

Marcie's Mob was a bunch of girls who were the best friends of an especially popular girl named Marcie. They could be a lot of fun, sitting together at lunch and hanging out between classes, laughing and talking about who was cool and who wasn't. Sometimes Marcie and her special friends let Xandra hang out with them, and sometimes they didn't. And when they didn't want you, they let you know it by the things they said and did. Things like glancing at Xandra and giggling, and mentioning crooked teeth or klutzy haircuts.

Not long after Belinda turned up in Mr. Fernandez's class, he sent her out of the room on a supposed errand so he could give a lecture about how a person shouldn't be judged on his or her appearance. And how he didn't want to see anyone teasing the new girl. After that Xandra lost interest in being on Belinda's side and began to join in the teasing when Mr. Fernandez wasn't looking. Not starting anything, but just going along with what other people were doing.

So it was really weird when Xandra found herself not only talking to Belinda, but telling her a little about the mysterious bird. It happened just before school started on the day the bird disappeared. Xandra, who had gotten to school early, was sitting on a bench in the outdoor lunch area, an unpopular spot on such a chilly morning. She was all alone and that was just the way she wanted it. She retrieved the white feather from its hiding place, hanging around her neck on a necklace of strong twine. She was running it back and forth across the palm of her hand when a voice said, "Oh, let me touch it. May I?" It was Belinda.

Dressed as usual in a ragged skirt and the incredibly awful jacket, Belinda reached out, not to touch the feather but only to hold her hand just above it, as if it could be felt without making contact. All Xandra could do was stare in shocked silence, but as she did she began to see some things she'd not noticed before. Belinda's eyes, for instance. Large eyes with strangely shaped irises, like the eyes of a cat on a dark night. And the rest of her face was unusual too. Not exceptionally beautiful or ugly, but with something strange about it that suddenly reminded Xandra of faces in some of the pictures that covered the walls of her room. Pictures of exotic-looking people in fantastical places. Shivering, Xandra turned away, covering the feather with her left hand.

"Why?" she asked. "Why should I let you touch it? It's mine. I found it."

Belinda nodded enthusiastically. "I know it's yours," she said. "But how did you get it? Did it just appear? Did it choose you somehow?"

Of course Xandra already knew that was how it had happened. The feather, and the bird it had come from, had chosen her in some mysterious way. But she was surprised and shocked to find that Belinda knew it too. Only a few minutes later she began to tell Belinda all about the beautiful wounded bird and how she had rescued it, fed it with brine shrimp and left it shut away in the safe and secure basement. And how in the morning it was gone, leaving behind the feather.

As Belinda listened, her strange eyes narrowed, widened and then narrowed again. "Could someone else have taken it, or scared it away?" she asked.

"No." Xandra spoke quickly and confidently. "No one else ever goes there."

"Oh? Are you sure? Maybe one of your brothers or sisters?"

Xandra shook her head, smiling grimly. "One of my siblings? Not a chance."

"Oh. But you do have . . . siblings?"

"Oh, sure." Xandra sighed and shrugged. "Dozens of them. But if they'd found the bird I would have known. They would have bragged about it."

Belinda looked slightly suspicious. "You have dozens of brothers and sisters? Really?"

Xandra shrugged again. "Who knows. I don't. I stopped counting a long time ago."

"Oh, I see." This time Belinda's nod was slow and thoughtful. "I guess it's for sure, then. There's no other way to explain it."

"To explain what?" Xandra asked.

"The feather." Belinda pointed to where Xandra was still holding the feather in one hand and covering it with the other. There was an excited whispery sound to her voice as she said, "It really must be a . . ." She paused.

"A what?" Xandra urged.

Belinda breathed deeply before she went on. "Well, different people call them different things but my . . ." She paused again. "Some people call them Keys." The word *keys* came out in a long and drawn-out whisper, so that Xandra wasn't sure just what she'd heard.

"Keys?" she asked.

Belinda nodded.

"Ke-e-e-ys to what?" Xandra asked, trying to draw out the word the way Belinda had done.

Belinda paused again before she whispered, "To another place. Well, not to another place, actually, but to where you can see things that most people can't see." Her voice trailed away into a quivering silence.

"Things other people can't see?" Xandra repeated under her breath as she opened her hands to stare at the feather. Stared at what, after all, was only a bunch of weightless white filaments attached to a long hollow stem. After a while she shrugged, and bouncing the feather on her open hands, she asked, "But how can a feather be a key?" Making a gesture as if she were turning a key in a lock, and trying for a sarcastic drawl, she said, "Let's see. How would that work?" But somehow the sarcasm she was trying for just didn't happen. Instead, her question sounded embarrassingly sincere.

Belinda's answer was, "I don't know, at least not for sure. I'm just beginning to learn about things like that. Other things besides feathers can be Keys, like old amulets and certain kinds of stones, but I have heard of a feather being a Key."

"But how?" Xandra asked. "I don't get it. It's such an ordinary little thing." She tossed the feather on her palm again, demonstrating how little it weighed. "I mean, there's nothing to it."

"Oh no," Belinda said. "There's nothing that's so strong for its size and weight. Just think how important they are to birds. I mean, for birds they're the key to a whole different element—a whole different dimension."

"Okay, okay," Xandra said, and now her tilted sarcastic smile was working again. "So, okay, having feathers is important for birds. But what can they—I mean what can this one do for me?" She made the key-in-the-lock motion again. "How is it going to open anything for me?"

Belinda didn't return the smile. She sounded serious—

deadly serious—as she began to answer. "I don't know; at least I don't know yet. I'm just beginning to find out more about things like that. I've only started to learn . . ."

Xandra frowned suspiciously. "How? How will you find out?" she asked.

"Well, I'll just ask my . . ." Belinda slowly shook her head and whispered, "There are lots of ways to learn things like that."

Before Xandra could ask what ways there were, the first bell rang and Belinda turned and walked quickly away. Xandra didn't try to follow her.

3

ALL THE REST of that day while she did ordinary things, Xandra's mind was full of the extraordinary. As she attended classes, rode home on the bus, changed out of her school uniform, her thoughts kept returning to the white feather and to what the girl named Belinda had said about it. And they went on returning there all the way through dinner, even though the scene at the Hobsons' dinner table on that night was also a bit out of the ordinary, if only because everybody was there for once. Everybody, including both parents, all the siblings, and even Clara, the babysitter, who often ate early with her five-year-old "baby," the youngest member of the Hobson family.

The dining room at the Hobson Habitat was very large. To Xandra's way of thinking, much too enormous to make any sense. She'd heard the parents excuse its size by saying that when they'd planned the house, they'd been thinking they would have time to give lots of large dinner parties. "Before we realized just how much time we'd have to spend on the increasing demands of career and family," Henry, the Hobson father, would say. Or Helen, the mother, would gesture to whatever family members happened to be present and raise one of her beautiful eyebrows as she said, "Or the demands of an *increasing* family."

So that night after Xandra arrived, late as usual, they were all there. Nine in all, counting Clara, spread out around a dining table that could easily have seated twenty, while Geraldine, the cook, brought in the food, thumped it down on the table and stomped out grumpily. Geraldine was always grumpy, but as Helen liked to tell people, "Good cooks are so hard to find, so we've chosen to put up with a certain amount of temperament."

Seated around such a long table, you needed to raise your voice quite a bit if you wanted to be heard. To shout almost. The first topic everyone was shouting about that evening was report cards. The first quarter of the school year was almost over and the Hobson siblings would soon find out how they were going to be graded in their new classes by new teachers. Everyone seemed to be looking forward to the experience. Everyone, that is, except Xandra.

Xandra wasn't looking forward to receiving her report card and she definitely had nothing to say on the subject. There was nothing unusual about that. The thing that was unusual that night was how easy it was for her to keep her mind on other things and not even notice what was being said around the table—to keep her mind on an enchanted white bird and a possibly miraculous feather, not to mention all the weird things the girl named Belinda had told her. So even when Quincy, the high school senior and owner of the fancy aquarium, practically shouted, "I'm pretty sure my grade point average is going to be the best yet," Xandra hardly bothered to notice how disgustingly smug and conceited he sounded. But then the little one shrieked in her high babyish voice, "You always get the best grades in the whole world, don't you, Quincy?" and the whole family laughed, even the adults.

Everybody laughed their heads off, including both the parents and even Clara, who, as a child-care expert, definitely should have known better. You'd think they'd realize that it was pretty stupid to encourage a five-year-old, who already was sure she was the cutest thing in the whole universe, to think she was also some kind of world-class comedian.

Even Clara. Xandra squinted as she concentrated on the chubby, smile-creased face of the woman who had been her own baby-sitter for almost seven years. The one who had held Xandra on her big soft lap every night while she read or made up stories, and who told everyone about the smart things Xandra said and did. And who then, seven years later, forgot all about everybody else when the beautiful new baby was born.

Not that it bothered Xandra anymore. Particularly not tonight when there were other thoughts and feelings that were so much more important. Thoughts about the strange things the girl named Belinda had said, and feelings like the mysteriously warm spot on her chest where the feather still hung around her neck.

Back in her room Xandra went directly toward her bed, passing quickly by the long bookshelves and all the posters and paintings. And passing even more quickly the glass-topped dressing table with its frilly skirt and three-way mirror.

The dressing table had not been Xandra's idea and she rarely looked at it. It was even rarer for her to look into its fancy gold-framed mirror. But now she suddenly turned back and sat down on the dressing table's bench as she slowly pulled the feather out from its hiding place under her blouse. Holding it in both hands, she stroked it gently, looking into the mirror to admire the downy fringe at the base of its blade. A fringe made up of such fine filaments that they seemed to be constantly quivering, even when she held her breath to keep from creating the slightest breeze. A continuous silent shiver that made the feather seem, in some mysterious way, a living thing. She was smiling as she held it up to her face, feeling the soft quiver of the filaments against her chin.

A kind of magical Key, Belinda had said, but she hadn't said what kind of magic it had or what it could do. As she thought about magical objects she had read or heard about, genies came to mind, and the granting of wishes. Usually it was three wishes. That was an interesting idea. Clutching the feather tightly in both hands, she closed her eyes and wished. Wished at first in an offhand, game-playing way, which turned into an almost serious plea for some very important differences. But when she opened her eyes, nothing had changed. The face in the mirror was still fat-cheeked, snaggletoothed and surrounded by dark brown hair that stuck out stubbornly in stiff ugly-looking chunks. Shoving the feather back under her blouse, she hurried to her bed and curled up among her animals.

Xandra's collection of animals was fairly large—forty-seven at last count. Stuffed toy animals, of course, although she never thought of them as toys. But clean and quiet as they obviously were, there were way too many of them, according to the rest of the family. Not to mention the opinion of every cleaning-service person who ever tried to do something about Xandra's room. But stuffed animals were one of the collections that had been growing throughout Xandra's life, along with books and pictures of enchanted places, and she wasn't about to part with a single picture or book or animal. Particularly not a single animal.

With her head resting on a hippo and her arms full of cats, dogs, tigers and teddy bears, she went on wondering and planning. Wondering about Belinda—who she was, and how much of what she said could be believed. And what she had meant when she'd called the feather a Key. Very soon, Xandra told herself, she would get the answers to all her questions. Like tomorrow morning, when she would be waiting for Belinda in the outdoor eating area.

❧ ❧ ❧

But it didn't happen quite that way. When Xandra awoke the next morning it was raining, and by the time she arrived at school the rain had turned into a downpour. So the outdoor lunch area was out of the question. And of course starting a conversation with Belinda in the hall, possibly in front of Marcie and her Mob, and a lot of other people, was more or less out of the question too.

Xandra was in the crowded hall putting some books in her locker and trying to decide what to do when someone brushed against her and she thought she felt a hand in her raincoat pocket. Slamming the locker door, she whirled around quickly enough to get a glimpse of a head of straggly dark hair and the back of a decrepit suit jacket disappearing into the crowd. She opened her mouth to call, "Belinda, come back," and shut it again. She started to follow Belinda down the hall and then, noticing that some of Marcie's close friends were watching, quickly came to a stop. She wasn't about to let the Mob see her running after the class weirdo. At last all she could do was reach into her pocket, where she found a tightly folded scrap of paper.

The note, written in a slanted script, was difficult to read but after careful study it was possible to make out,

WAIT UNTIL 3:30 AND THEN CATCH THE B2 BUS TO THE DOWNTOWN BUS TERMINAL. I'LL BE ON THE BUS AND WE CAN TALK.

Instead of a signature there was a tiny picture of a bee. Obviously Bee for Belinda.

That seemed to be it. Xandra felt angry and frustrated. She didn't know if she wanted to sit with Belinda on the bus. What she had to consider was whether the risk was worthwhile. The risk that someone she knew would see her sitting with such a freakish person. She still hadn't decided whether she was going to do it or not when a few minutes later, in the classroom, she happened to catch Belinda's eye and found herself nodding. Nodding to say yes, she would be there. On the B2 bus at 3:30.

Xandra was the only one of all the Hobson siblings who regularly rode the city bus. Quincy had started driving to school in his own car, and the others usually got rides in carpools driven by the parents of their Heritage Avenue friends, and once in a while, when it was the Hobson family's turn, by Clara. But Xandra wasn't the carpooler type. So what if it was faster and maybe a little more comfortable? She'd tried it just once and that was enough. After she'd been teased or ignored all the way to school by older siblings and their friends, the bus seemed like a better choice, even if she did have to pay for it out of her own allowance. But this time, instead of catching the 3:15 that went straight to Heritage Avenue, she would be taking the B2, which headed for the downtown bus terminal, where she could transfer to one that went to Heritage Avenue.

The B2 bus left a little later, so Xandra got to the stop early, and at first there was no sign of Belinda. When she did show up, she didn't say hello or even seem to notice that Xandra was there. It wasn't until the bus had arrived and Xandra had taken a seat near the rear that Belinda came down the aisle and sat beside her.

For a minute or two they only glanced at each other and quickly turned away, but then, still looking in the other direction, Belinda whispered, "Where is it?"

"Where is what?" Xandra began, and then answered her own question: "Oh, that. Here it is." She began to pull up on the string. "Under my blouse."

"No. Don't take it out. Not here." Belinda was looking at her now. "Just tell me again about how you found the bird. And what you did with it when you got home."

So Xandra went over the story again, and when she got

to the part about the basement, she somehow started telling other things. Some very private things she'd never told anyone before. Right there on the noisy, bumpy bus, she began to tell Belinda about all the animals she'd raised and doctored in her basement hideout. Afterward she wasn't sure just how or why that had happened. Of course, Belinda had seemed very interested and asked a lot of questions. And, as Xandra told herself later, how much Belinda knew didn't really matter, because it wasn't as if she would have a chance to visit the basement, or to tell any of Xandra's friends or family about the private things she'd learned.

In fact, Xandra did so much talking that first day, she didn't get around to finding out anything more about the feather. She'd just managed to ask Belinda to tell her more about Keys when the bus pulled into the terminal, where Xandra had to catch the Heritage Avenue/Downtown bus while Belinda ran to catch the one that went into the country toward the west.

4

FROM THEN ON Xandra and Belinda met on the bus every day. The trip into the town center took only about twenty minutes, but as Xandra soon discovered, a lot of important things can be discussed in just twenty minutes.

On the second day Xandra again did most of the talking, telling Belinda more about particular animals that had lived in the basement. About funny little Stinky, who had sometimes threatened by stomping his feet and lifting his tail, but who had never really let her have it. And about some of the kittens she had kept for a while before advertising them in the local humane society's newspaper and finding them good homes. And about Ratchet, the baby barn owl.

On another bus ride a day or two later, Belinda asked, "Did you have to give away all the kittens? Didn't you ever get to keep one of them for your own?"

"Well, not for very long." Xandra shrugged as she said, "And certainly not to take into the house. My dad is allergic to animals—at least that's what he says. And my mother has a phobia about them because something bit her when she was a baby, or some such story, but I think it's mostly because they shed."

Belinda's smile looked sympathetic, but when Xandra asked her whether her parents let her have pets, her eyes narrowed and she looked away. "I don't have parents," she said, "except for my grandfather. He likes animals and we used to have a dog and three cats before—before we had to move."

When Xandra asked, "But you don't have any pets now?" Belinda only shook her head.

"No, except for a squirrel," she said. "And a feral barn cat that I've started to tame. But I'll have a dog again someday. My grandfather thinks animals are very important. All kinds of animals. My grandfather says animals are like . . . messengers."

The animals-as-messengers concept caught Xandra's attention, because she'd had some ideas along those lines herself. And she was intrigued by the interesting fact that Belinda didn't have any family except a grandfather. But she soon discovered that Keys and what they were good for was a subject Belinda seemed more and more reluctant to discuss.

On some days they discussed books, and the other kids who went to Carter Academy. When the subject was books, Belinda's eyes got their cat-at-midnight look and she would talk and talk, telling which were her favorites and why, and which ones she owned herself and had read over and over. Some of her favorites were Xandra's too, such as the books about the Borrowers, all the stories about Narnia, the Green Knowe books by Lucy Boston, and everything by J.R.R. Tolkien.

But about people at school, like the Marcie Mob girls for instance, Belinda had little to say. When Xandra talked about how popular the Mob girls were, and how mean and snobbish they could be, Belinda would only say she hadn't noticed. But she always seemed interested in what Xandra had to say about almost any subject that happened to come up. As the days went by, it began to seem that the only things Belinda would not discuss were anything that had to do with her grandfather, and the Key.

One day after Xandra had asked her for the umpteenth time what she had learned about the Key and Belinda had changed the subject, Xandra said, "Okay, Belinda. What's going on? You said you were going to find out more about my feather or Key or whatever it is and tell me all about it. And now you won't even talk about it."

"I know." Belinda sighed and shook her head. "It's just that . . . Well, I guess I decided I shouldn't say anything more about it until I find out . . ." She paused, looking at Xandra through narrowed eyes. "More about you, I guess, and how you happened to get it."

"More about me?" Xandra knew her voice sounded pretty frustrated. "You have to know more about me? I don't know what else I can tell you. I've told you more about me than I've ever told anybody. What else can I tell you?"

Staring at Xandra, Belinda shook her head slowly but

then suddenly her eyes widened. "I don't know really, but maybe if I could see the place where you found it, I would be able to tell if . . ."

"Where I found the bird?" Xandra said. "But I don't know if I can. I told you I'm not supposed to go into the forest—"

"No, no," Belinda interrupted. "I don't mean where you found the bird. I mean the Key. Where you found the Key."

"You mean—you mean the basement?"

Cat-eyed, and strangely intent, Belinda nodded.

"But why? How would that help?"

"I'm not sure, but my grandfather . . . I mean, some people think that where you find a Key is an important sign."

They were almost to the downtown station and Xandra had to think quickly. If they approached the house from the back, it wasn't likely that anyone would notice them, and Belinda probably wouldn't stay very long. "All right," she said. "When we get to the terminal you can just get on the Heritage Avenue bus with me and—"

"Oh, not today," Belinda interrupted. "First I'll have to tell my grandfather that I'll be late."

That seemed like an easily solved problem. "Couldn't you call him from the station?" Xandra asked.

Belinda shook her head. "No," she said. "There's no phone where we live. Could we do it tomorrow?"

Busy picturing what it would be like to live without a telephone, Xandra nodded. "All right," she said. "Tomorrow will be all right." But later that evening a problem arose that made her wonder if it would be possible.

When Xandra arrived at the Hobson dinner table that night, almost on time for once, Clara was there, and all the siblings, but that was all. No parents. Nothing very un-usual about that, of course. Most of the time one or both of the parents were away at dinnertime. But tonight the reason for Helen's, the mother's, absence was slightly out of the ordinary. That evening Helen Hobson, the famous trial lawyer, was going to be on television on the evening news. So everybody ate quickly and took their desserts into the family room, even Quincy, who, as a privileged eighteen-year-old, could have watched in his own room.

And then there she was, Helen Hobson, talking about the important case she was working on and how obvious it was that her client was going to win. And then the reporters were asking her questions and she was joking with them and doing her famous arched eyebrow and dazzling smile, and Quincy and the other siblings were saying things like "Yeah, knock 'em dead, Mom." And "That's telling them."

But then the rest of the news came on and Clara and her "baby" left and the rest of them sat around for a while listening to stuff about the weather and what was going on in Washington. Xandra was the next one to leave, and that was when the problem that could have fouled up Belinda's visit began to happen.

Xandra had closed the door firmly behind her and was headed for the window seat when she came to a sudden stop and whirled around to stare at the closet door. Someone or something was moving around inside her closet, thumping and shuffling and then bursting out through the door, as Xandra stood motionless, frozen in shocked surprise that quickly changed to anger. It was only Augusta, or Darling Little Gussie, as most people called the youngest of the Hobson siblings. As she stumbled out of the closet, Gussie's curly blond hair was a bushy tangle and her big baby-doll blue eyes were wide and unblinking.

At first, while she was still recovering from the scare, Xandra could only stammer, "Wh-what are you doing in my closet?"

Gussie was smiling now, a little shakily. "I was just . . ." She paused then before she went on in a questioning tone of voice, "I was . . . maybe I was . . . walking in my sleep?"

"Sure you were," Xandra snarled. "You think I'm going to believe that?" And then, noticing a suspicious bulge under Gussie's bathrobe, "What's that under your robe?"

Reaching under her bathrobe, Gussie pulled out an alligator, one of Xandra's favorite animals, and held it out toward Xandra's bed. "I know I promised I wouldn't play with your animals again and I wasn't playing with it, not really. I was just . . . I was just looking at it a little. I was just getting ready to put it back on your bed."

"Yeah, I'll bet you were," Xandra said. "I guess that's why you were hiding in my closet with my alligator hidden under your robe?"

Gussie tried for the cutesy dimpling smile that got her out of trouble with most people. But it wasn't going to work with Xandra. Particularly not this time, when she'd been up to something she'd done before and had promised she was going to stop doing.

"I didn't hide," she whimpered. "I didn't hide until you were coming and I was scared. And I didn't hide the alligator. It hid under my robe 'cause it was scared too."

Before she could go on, Xandra had her by the shoulders and was shaking her so hard that her curly hair flipped and flopped like a shaken dust mop.

"I've told you and told you to stay out of my things, Gussie Hobson," Xandra said through clenched teeth. "Do you hear me, you little brat?"

"Okay. Okay. Don't hurt me." Gussie looked terrified. "Here, take it back. Take back your old alligator." Pulling away from Xandra's grasp, Gussie almost, but not quite, ducked the slap Xandra aimed at her as she threw the alligator on the floor and ran from the room.

As Xandra watched her go, she knew she was in trouble. The little creep would tell on her for sure and probably lie about it too. She'd probably say that Xandra hit her, which wasn't true—at least not exactly. Maybe she had more or less tried to hit the little troublemaker, but she was pretty sure she had mostly missed. But if Gussie said she'd been hit, there was going to be trouble. People tended to believe the worst about Xandra, and the best about their Darling Little Gussie. Even their mother, who, as a lawyer, wasn't supposed to make up her mind about who was guilty without hearing all the evidence. The chances were Xandra would be grounded, which meant Clara would pick her up after school and she'd have to go straight to her room and stay there all evening. So there would be no way she could smuggle Belinda into the basement.

She went back to the window seat and threw herself onto it, thinking about how unfair it was going to be. Gussie would tell her side of the story, and the whole family, all the siblings as well as the parents, would be mad at Xandra and she'd probably get some horrible punishment, like having her allowance cut in half, besides being grounded for a whole week.

5

XANDRA WENT DOWNSTAIRS the next morning expecting the worst, but to her surprise nothing was said about what she'd done, or hadn't done, to Gussie. Nothing at all. Of course they were all in their usual rush to get to work and to school, but that didn't really explain it. The only explanation, Xandra decided, was that Gussie just hadn't gotten around to telling yet. Of course, that didn't mean she wouldn't as soon as she had a good chance. But then again, maybe nothing more would be said about it. Xandra didn't mention the Gussie problem the next morning when Belinda whispered that, yes, she could go home with Xandra after school.

That afternoon the bus ride was strangely quiet. Two bus rides, actually—downtown as usual and then the transfer. "No. I can't," Xandra had said when Belinda had asked if they would be taking the 3:15 bus that went directly to Heritage Avenue. "I have a bunch of stuff to do after class, so I'll probably be too late. Let's take the downtown bus, like always. Okay?"

Belinda said okay, and later on the bus she didn't ask any questions about the time-consuming things Xandra had supposedly been doing. She didn't, in fact, say much of anything and neither did Xandra. Xandra was busy thinking about things she didn't feel like mentioning, like for instance the real reason she hadn't wanted to take the Heritage Avenue bus, where she would probably have seen other kids she knew. The time passed slowly until the second bus came to a stop and there they were, standing on the Heritage Avenue sidewalk only about three short blocks from the Hobsons' house.

Glancing around quickly to see if anyone was watching, and then feeling embarrassed about doing it, Xandra said, "So, what you want to see is just the place where I found the feather? Right?"

"Oh yes." Belinda's eyes widened. "Can we go there right now? Right away?"

Xandra nodded. "Sure we can." She paused, looking around as if trying to make up her mind. "Well, there are a couple of ways to get there from here. We could go right on up Heritage Avenue, or we could take this shortcut. Well, actually it's more of a long-cut, but it's a lot more interesting. It goes down Wildwood for a block or two and then through the edge of the forest. Which way would you like to go?"

What she didn't mention was that the first way would lead past the homes of several people she knew, and then right down the Hobsons' driveway, where, at this time of day, someone would be sure to see them. She didn't mention it, but she somehow had an uncomfortable feeling that she might as well have. Belinda's level gaze lasted a moment too long before she said, "You choose. You must know the best way to get there."

So that was why they started off down Wildwood, where, after the first house or two, there were mostly vacant lots before the road ended in a graveled path that led into the forest. Into an acre or two of young second-growth trees, where the road dwindled away just before it reached the edge of the deep forest.

They didn't talk much at first; in fact Belinda tended to hang back, walking a few steps behind Xandra, but as they reached the trees, she caught up and said, "I thought you said the reason you couldn't take me to where you found the bird was because you weren't supposed to go into the forest."

Xandra nodded. "That's what I said, but I meant I wasn't supposed to go very far into it, and this way we don't have to. We're just going to go up here along the edge of the trees and then we'll cut back toward the houses. We're almost there now." And then to change the subject she stopped to point out a dangerous hornets' nest, and a little farther along, the remains of a mockingbird's nest. And that led to telling about the baby mockingbird.

When she told about rescuing and raising a baby mockingbird that had fallen out of the nest, Belinda's cool disinterest faded away. "We do that sometimes," she said eagerly. "We rescue baby birds."

"We?" Xandra asked. "You and your grandfather?"

Belinda nodded. "Yes," she said. "Me and my grandfather. He's very good at finding baby birds and raising them."

Xandra waited, hoping to hear more about what the grandfather was good at, but Belinda only turned away and went on walking. They were almost through the grove of small trees when Belinda asked, "Do any of your brothers and sisters"—she paused long enough to let her smile say she remembered what Xandra called them—"I mean your siblings, like the forest? I mean, do they go there with you?"

"No," Xandra said quickly and firmly. "Not with *me* anyway. Two of them, the two that are twins, go exploring in the forest sometimes, just because they aren't supposed to. And just so they can try to scare me by pretending to be experts about all sorts of dangerous things that might live there. Things like snakes and mountain lions."

Belinda nodded. "Oh yes," she said. "I think I heard about your twin brothers. I heard some girls talking about them in the cafeteria."

Xandra wasn't surprised. She was used to hearing girls rave about what great jocks and how cute her twin brothers were. She shrugged and sighed. "Yeah," she said. "All the girls are crazy about them, but all I can say is, they can have them."

She might have had more sarcastic things to say about her "gorgeous" twin brothers, but just about then they reached the place where the path led out of the forest and right up to the Hobsons' back gate. Up to the gate, then, after a careful check to be sure no one was in the yard—no Hobson siblings and not even Otto, the gardener—Xandra quickly led the way across the lawn, around flower and herb beds, and then they were there. Right there in the basement, where the white bird had disappeared, leaving behind the enchanted feather.

Nothing had changed since the miraculous disappearance of the bird. Once inside the door, they had to make their way through the huge storage room among the boxes and trunks and all kinds of sports and household equipment, including every kind of vacuum cleaner that had ever been invented. As Xandra led the way through the piles of junk, Belinda hung back, looking from side to side. She seemed interested in all of it, particularly the vacuum cleaners. "Broken?" she asked. "Are they *all* broken?"

"Some of them might be." Xandra shrugged. "My mother kept getting different kinds, hoping somebody in the family would get interested in using them. But finally she just gave up and hired a cleaning service." She shrugged again. "Come on. What we came to see is back here."

It was then, while Belinda was hanging back to inspect the vacuum cleaners, that Xandra began to have some serious second thoughts. Here she was letting an almost perfect stranger in on one of the most important secrets of her whole life. A stranger who at the moment seemed more interested in boring housecleaning stuff than in secret hideouts and enchanted creatures.

"Why?" Xandra asked herself. "Why should I let her in on my secrets?" But right then, while she was still whispering the question, she knew the answer. Or perhaps felt it more than knew it. Felt the answer as a feathery warmth against the skin of her chest. Putting her hand over the spot where, beneath her blouse, the feather hung on its string, she nodded. Belinda was there because of what she had said and done when she saw the feather. How she had known immediately how important it was, and how, before Xandra had told her anything, she had begun to talk about Keys and who got them and what they could do.

So instead of trying to get rid of Belinda, Xandra pulled firmly on the back of her ratty old jacket. "Come on," she said. "We're not there yet. You have to duck under those heat vents first and then go on around behind the furnace."

At last Belinda tore herself away from the vacuum cleaners and followed Xandra back into the dimly lit area where in cages of different shapes and sizes all Xandra's orphaned and wounded creatures had lived. And where now, as always, she immediately began to feel better, calmer and less impatient.

"Well, here we are," she started to say when she noticed that Belinda was staring, looking from side to side in a strange, intense way. In the dim light her wide-set eyes glowed with excitement, or fear, or maybe some of each.

"You kept all your animals here?" she asked. "Without anybody knowing?"

Xandra shrugged. "Well, mostly they didn't know. Or didn't care—at least not as long as they didn't have to do anything about it."

"And where are they now, the animals?" Belinda whispered.

"Some of them, like the kittens, I found homes for. Like I told you, some of my family are allergic, so I couldn't have them in the house. But most of the rest of them just grew up or got well and flew away or ran away into the forest. And I let the wild ones go on purpose, at least more or less.

I don't think wild things ought to be penned up. Anyway, what you came to see, the place where I found the feather, is right over there. In that box."

Xandra approached the empty carton slowly and solemnly. "Here it is," she told Belinda. "See, the bowls are still there. This one was for water, and this one had brine shrimp in it. I haven't moved anything since . . ." She paused and then went on dramatically. "Since the white bird disappeared into thin air."

Belinda reached out slowly and carefully to touch the bowls, one after the other. Then she put her hand, palm down, on the straw at the center of the box. "Is this where it sat? Where it left the feather?"

Xandra nodded.

Belinda raised her hand, studied the spot where it had been, and then looked around the basement. "And the door was still closed the next morning when the bird was gone?"

Xandra nodded again.

Belinda turned in a slow circle and then came to a stop. "And the feather?" she asked. "You still have it?"

Xandra put her hand over the spot on her chest where she could feel the feather's shimmering warmth. "Of course," she said. "It's still right here on this string."

Belinda held out both hands and slowly and carefully Xandra pulled the string over her head and even more slowly put the feather into Belinda's hands.

As Xandra produced the enchanted feather, she was feeling uncertain and more than a little doubtful. She watched carefully through narrowed eyes as Belinda held the feather, staring down to where it lay across her two hands. She went on staring for so long that Xandra began to be impatient.

"What's the matter?" she asked finally. "Why don't you do something?"

Belinda shook her head slowly. "I don't know." Her voice was faint, almost fearful. "I'm not sure if we should try. I'm not sure if I know enough yet."

"Yet?" Xandra couldn't keep the impatience out of her voice. "What do you mean, yet?"

"I'm just learning," Belinda said. "He began to teach me and then . . ."

"He?" Xandra demanded. "Who is he?"

Belinda's eyes moved to Xandra's face and then quickly flicked away.

"So tell me," Xandra went on. "Who was teaching you? Do you mean your grandfather? What is he, some kind of wizard, or like that?"

"No." Belinda's answer was quick and indignant. "Don't say that. He's not a wizard. He's a . . ." She turned her face away and for a long moment said nothing at all. But then, watching her carefully, Xandra noticed that her expression was changing as she stared down at the feather that still lay across her hands.

Suddenly Belinda breathed deeply, and enclosing the feather in both hands, she raised them over her head and then pressed the feather against her forehead. She held it there for a long minute before she slowly took it away and stared at Xandra.

"What is it? What happened?" Xandra asked urgently, but Belinda only shook her head. "Nothing," she whispered. "Nothing happened because it isn't mine. But if you did it . . ." She grabbed Xandra's hand and put the feather in it.

"Now you," she said. "Hold it between your hands and raise them like this. Now put the feather on your forehead."

Xandra did as she was told. Holding the feather between her hands, she raised them over her head and then pressed the feather to her forehead. She held it there as time passed—an amount of time that was too short to measure yet seemed to stretch out into a timeless forever. At last, out of that far distant forever, Xandra heard

Belinda's voice calling her name, asking, "Xandra. Did you feel it? Did you feel something happening?"

"I don't know," Xandra started to say, and then suddenly she did. It was as if something was moving and stretching inside her eyes. Only her eyes at first and then deep into her whole face, her ears, her nose, and then her hands and fingers as well. When the sensation began to fade, it left her feeling confused and bewildered. "What happened?" she whispered. "What happened to me? Do I look different?"

"Your eyes," Belinda whispered back. "They're different. The dark part is bigger. Did it hurt?"

"No," Xandra said uncertainly. "No, not exactly. There was just a feeling. Like a swelling and a kind of tingle." She turned her head from one side to the other and then whispered, "Look. Look over there. And there too."

"Where. At what?" Belinda asked. "What are you seeing?"

Xandra looked again but for a brief moment there was nothing. At least nothing she hadn't seen a hundred times before—except that . . .

There she was in her own private hideout, where every object was completely familiar, and for the first few moments everything looked the same as it always had—except that everything, every cage and cupboard and box, suddenly seemed to have clear, almost transparent surfaces. And beneath the surfaces there seemed to be an endless shimmering movement, as if the atoms and molecules had somehow become visible.

Fascinated by the new glitter and gleam of ordinary objects, Xandra needed a minute to become aware of some less familiar, and less stationary, shapes. And when she did begin to notice them, they at first seemed to be nothing more than moving shadows. Shadows that looked like small clumps of darkness that constantly changed in shape and color as they moved nearer and then faded away.

There were smells too, and noises. The familiar musty animal odors of pen and cage were stronger now, among them the warm, milky scent of young kittens. The sounds were familiar too, chirps and clucks and clicks and soft growls and grunts. And now, little by little, some of the moving shadows were coming nearer and taking on more recognizable shapes.

Startled and a little frightened, Xandra began to back away. "Look," she said. "It's like there's something over there that keeps moving. Like dark fuzzy clouds that keep moving around. Do you see them? What are they?"

Belinda was right beside her. "I don't see them," she said. "What do they look like?" Ignoring Belinda's question, Xandra was bending down and putting out her hand, reaching out until she almost seemed to touch the nearest cloudy blur. Reaching out, and then suddenly snatching her hand away.

"How did it feel?" Belinda asked. "Did it hurt your fingers when you touched it?"

Xandra shook her head. "No, not hurt. But I could feel it. I could feel a difference—like a shivering. A kind of aliveness. Just a kind of warm aliveness. Everything feels alive, and there are noises too. Don't you hear anything?"

"Noises?" Belinda cocked her head, listening. "No, not really. What do they sound like?"

"A kind of soft buzzing noise, like tiny motors. Or like

purring. Like purring kittens," Xandra said. "And bird sounds too. Like birds chirping and a kind of clicking noise. Like . . ." She paused. "Like running a stick along fence posts."

Belinda was nodding. "The baby owl?" she asked.

"Yes," Xandra whispered excitedly. "Like the noise Ratchet made when he wanted to be fed." She was turning in a circle, trying to tell where the sounds were coming from, when she noticed something else. A familiar musty warning odor that most people hated but that could be quite interesting when it wasn't too strong. "Look. Look over there," she said.

"Where?" Belinda asked.

"Something over there on the floor, by that big box. I see it." As Xandra moved toward the box, Belinda was beside her talking excitedly. "Does it look like an animal?" she said. "When I told my grandfather about your Key he said that things like animals were what you might see. Animals like the ones you took care of. Only with the Key they would be animals from the Unseen."

"From the Unseen? What does that mean? Is it a place?"

"It's . . . well, it's . . ." Belinda was stumbling. "It's not really a place, because it's everywhere, all the time, only most people can't see it." Shrugging and throwing out her hands helplessly, she went on, "I don't know how to tell you."

"Animals from the Unseen?" Xandra murmured questioningly as she moved forward and knelt down on the dusty floor next to a big carton. The musty smell was stronger now and very familiar. She reached out toward something that kept emerging from behind the box and then fading back behind it. A something that might have looked very familiar if parts of it hadn't kept blurring in and out of sight. Parts like a pointed black nose, a white-striped back and tail and black, beady eyes. Its cool little nose was snuffling gently over Xandra's hand when it suddenly stilled, dimmed and faded away behind the box.

As Xandra got to her feet, Belinda was standing beside her. "Did you see him?" Xandra asked excitedly. "I think it was Stinky. You know, the baby skunk I raised. He ran away a long time ago but I think he's come back. Only he's . . ." She paused. "Only he's different."

"Yes, yes, it's all different. Changing." Belinda had moved back to where she could peer out around the furnace. There was a sharp intensity to her voice, and her face had stiffened into a nervous mask. "Different," she repeated. "Something is changing." She grabbed Xandra's arm. "Maybe we've seen enough for now. I think we ought to get out of here."

"Go? Why?" Xandra was disappointed. "I'd like to see some other things, like maybe there will be some of my birds, and the garter snake. I had a pet garter snake once."

"I know. You told me." Belinda still seemed distracted and anxious. "I don't know," she said. "It's just that something out there in the other room is changing. I didn't feel it at first but now it seems to be getting worse. I can feel it, like in the air. A feeling in the air that just isn't . . . the way it should be."

"The air?" Xandra said. "What's wrong with the air?" She sniffed and then grinned. "Smells all right to me, or not any worse than usual anyway. I smelled Stinky a little while ago. But only a little bit. I always liked his smell as long as it wasn't too strong."

She stopped and sniffed again. And then suddenly she, too, was aware of a difference. And the smells were a part of it. A strange smoky odor that made her nostrils burn and her throat stiffen seemed to be drifting in, blotting out the soft musky smell of baby animals.

"Come on. We have to go." Belinda was grabbing her arm and pulling her from behind the furnace to where she could see out through the storage area and on to the basement door. "Look, what do you see now? Look over there."

Xandra looked but there was nothing to see. Nothing at all. Not even the boxes and trunks that had always been there. It was as if everything had suddenly been swallowed up into thick dark clumps of shadow. Strange blobs of darkness that seemed to come not so much from a lack of light, but as if the dark was flowing out from its own center, ballooning outward to engulf everything around it. There were sounds and smells too. Grinding, growling, rasping noises and strange, disgusting smells, Smells like dead things, and the burnt-out scent of wet ashes.

As Xandra began to move toward the basement door, pulled along by Belinda, the black haze grew and spread around them. And now, as the clumps grew larger, they became more transparent so that it was possible to see what they had been hiding. To see that what had seemed a dense, empty fog was actually alive with a crowded confusion of moving shapes that formed and reformed in the surrounding pools of darkness. Faded and then reappeared, becoming more and more distinct.

And then the vague bulges were forming into recognizable shapes. Some of them now seemed to resemble vaguely human forms, hunchbacked and heavy-headed, while others were only surging bulges that oozed along the floor like enormous ugly worms. But all of them, the almost-human figures as well as the worm-shaped ones, now seemed to have faces. Faces that were only empty ovals except for fiery red eyes above dark gaping mouths. Enormous, wide-open mouths that grew larger moment by moment as they shut and opened again. Then the faces were everywhere, faces with fiery eyes and enormous mouths edged with sharp slashes of glittering light.

As Xandra stared in wonder, she became aware of Belinda's hands on her arms, pulling her away from the swirling, heaving darkness. "Can you see them? What are they?" Xandra gasped.

"I can't see them," Belinda whispered, "but I think I know why they're here. I think they're dangerous." Her voice was louder and more urgent as she went on. "We have to get out of here, right now."

"Yes, let's get out." Xandra turned toward the basement door. "Here. This way. Come this way."

But now the clumps were there too. The swarming black cloud was all around them, surging pools of darkness, full of fiery eyes and cavernous mouths. Xandra was turning in a circle, looking frantically for an escape route, for a gap in the surrounding circle of mouths and eyes, when she became aware that Belinda was whispering, "The Key, Xandra. Where is it?"

"The Key?" Xandra gasped, and then, "Oh, the feather."

Pulling it over her head, she pressed it into Belinda's hands. "Can you do it? Can you get us out of here?"

"I don't know. I don't think I can," Belinda whispered as she took the feather. She held it in both hands, raised it over her head and then pressed it against her forehead. Nothing changed except that the threatening mouths moved in closer, and the angry grinding, grunting sounds grew louder. And then Xandra began to smell their hot breath and feel it on her bare legs and arms.

"Hurry, hurry, they're breathing on me," Xandra screamed. Her scream turned into shrieks of pain as needle-sharp fangs began to sink into her bare skin, on her legs first and then moving up to her arms as she threw them up to protect her face. The pain was sharp and deep and she could feel the hot blood oozing out and running down her legs and arms. She was still screaming when Belinda pressed the feather into her hands and guided them up over her head and then against her forehead. As Belinda pushed her forward, the dark clouds began to fade and pull away, and suddenly she was stumbling out through the open door. Out into daylight and fresh air. "Where did they go?" Xandra gasped. "What happened? What did you do? Was it the feather?"

"It was." Belinda's voice was faint and uncertain. "It was the Key. Your Key. You were the one who did it." She slammed the basement door behind them. "Are you all right?"

"All right? No, I'm not all right." Xandra's voice was still pitched at the edge of a scream. "They bit me. See, they bit me all . . ." Her high-pitched shriek faded away to nothing as she began to realize that the pain was gone. All of it—gone. And the wounds, the terrible deep wounds, were . . . She bent to run her hands over her smooth unbitten ankles. And all the blood? It was gone too. "But they bit me," she said. "It was horrible." She straightened up to stare at Belinda. "Didn't they bite you?"

Belinda looked uncertain. "No," she said. "I don't think they bit me." She looked down at her legs. "But I could tell what was happening to you."

It made no sense. Xandra stared at Belinda angrily. "It can't be real," she said. "Things don't happen like that. You don't get big holes chewed in you and all that blood, and then it's all healed over in just a minute."

"I know," Belinda said. "I don't understand it." She paused, frowning and shaking her head. "I'll find out, though. He should have told me what might happen. He should have told me more about what to do."

"You mean your grandfather?"

Belinda's eyes flicked to Xandra's face and then as quickly shifted away. "Never mind," she said. "But I think I can find out about . . . about what happened. I can tell you more about it after I have a chance to . . ." She nodded. "Yes, maybe then. But until I find out, you'd better . . ." Reaching out, she snatched the feather out of Xandra's hand.

She turned quickly and started back down the path that led to the back gate. Xandra ran after her. "Wait," she said. "My feather. Give me back my feather."

But Belinda shook her head as she clutched the feather against her chest.

"No. No, I mustn't. You mustn't. It's too dangerous."

"But it's mine."

Belinda continued to shake her head. "Promise not to ever do that again. Because next time it might be much worse. Like maybe the Key would stop working, and you wouldn't be able to escape."

"Escape? Escape from what? From where?"

Belinda's eyes widened. "From the Unseen," she said.

"The Unseen?" Xandra's voice was a shaky whisper. Somehow it was a frightening, really terrifying thought. "All right," she said. "I promise. I absolutely promise not to use it again unless you're here to help me. Okay?"

"Okay," Belinda repeated as she slowly and reluctantly put the feather back in Xandra's hands. "I guess it will be all right—if you keep your promise." But then she grabbed Xandra's wrist. Narrowing her eyes, she whispered, "Don't do anything at all until I find out about . . ." Her voice faded to silence, and turning away, she continued down the path, through the gate and out into the woods. Xandra watched her go before she headed for the house. At the bottom of the back steps she came to a stop. With one hand on the railing she turned to look toward the basement door.

Firmly closed now, and gleaming white in the rays of the afternoon sun, the basement door looked like . . . well, like the rest of the Hobsons' house, strong and sleek and sturdily built. But behind the door . . . Xandra shuddered. Turning quickly, she ran up the steps.

7

As SHE HURRIED up the back steps, Xandra was thinking only of getting to a safe place where she could think calmly about what had happened—or at least what seemed to have happened. To where she would be able to figure out what had really been going on—and how it could seem so absolutely real—and why. Something seemed to be telling her that figuring out the *why* of it was going to be very important. The why, and maybe most important of all, how much Belinda had to do with it. Belinda—or maybe the mysterious grandfather she always seemed to be not quite mentioning.

As she entered the back hallway, Xandra stopped long enough to nod firmly and with a great deal of determination. Yes, she would see Belinda at school and on the bus tomorrow and she would find out what had really happened in the basement. But in the meantime she would try to come to some sort of understanding of it by herself in the safety and quiet of her own room.

With the enchanted feather safely back around her neck, carefully hidden under her blouse, she was on her way up the stairs to her room when she began to realize that there was one thing that needed to be attended to first. A minor detour, but a very urgent one, had to be made immediately. The problem was that she was suddenly terribly hungry. She swallowed hard. She was, in fact, absolutely ravenous. Hungrier probably than she'd ever been in her entire life. Which actually wasn't too surprising, under the circumstances. Coming that close to being eaten alive was probably enough to make anyone hungry. Changing course, Xandra headed for the kitchen. For the kitchen first and foremost and for something substantial and solidly comforting to eat.

But a moment later, back downstairs and approaching the door, she became aware that the kitchen was already occupied. Occupied, judging by the sound of the voices, by a particular sibling and some of her friends. Along with such kitchen noises as the clatter and clank of plates and glasses and the slamming of the refrigerator door, she was hearing wave after wave of teenage chatter and laughter. Her hand was on the doorknob and she was steeling herself to join a bunch of giggling, shrieking teenage refrigerator raiders when a different sound forced her to back off entirely.

The new voice was a younger one and easily recognizable. High-pitched and as cutesy as a movie star kid's, the voice had to be Gussie's. Xandra winced. If the little rat hadn't already tattled about being shaken and yelled at, she would be sure to the moment Xandra showed up. Now that she had a large adoring audience, she'd be sure to whine about how she'd been mistreated. Xandra paused, undecided, and then gave up. Even if she only so much as dropped by for a moment to grab an apple or a cookie, things were certain to become horribly embarrassing. Hungry and angry, Xandra turned away, crept up the back stairs and headed for her room.

She was nearly there, passing the room of one of the twin siblings, when an alternative to immediate starvation occurred to her. The room belonged to the twin named Nicholas—one of the two siblings who were not only great at all sorts of athletics but also famous for their looks. Bulging with muscles, with mouths full of shiny white teeth and heads covered with thick curly hair, they looked, according to some of the girls at Carter Academy, like Greek gods. As far as Xandra was concerned the Greek-god stuff was ridiculous. Besides, she really resented the fact that she never could tell whether girls she knew, like Marcie and her friends, really liked her, or whether they were only being nice to her now and then because they were hoping she might introduce them to her "Greek-god" siblings.

But at the moment, the most interesting thing about this particular twin was that he had a tendency to collect a lot of other things besides sport trophies and stupid girl-friends. Nothing as fascinating as Quincy's exotic fish, actually, but some other fairly interesting junk, including, for instance, one or two of every kind of candy bar known to the civilized world.

Xandra had known about the candy bar collection ever since one day the summer before. She'd been hanging out in

Nicholas's room after he and Nelson, the other twin, had gone, as usual, to some sort of ball game. She hadn't exactly been snooping. At least that wasn't how she thought of it. Just checking out some of Nicholas's other more or less interesting collections, such as all kinds of books about Sherlock Holmes and other famous detectives. And she had just happened to come across, at the back of his closet, a huge box full of candy bars. Not just the wrappers—the bars themselves. A really big box full of all kinds of candy bars.

Why would anyone collect that many candy bars? But another question had occurred to her on that day, and that was whether Nicholas kept careful track of his collection. Careful enough to know if one was missing. She hadn't quite gotten up her nerve to test the answer to that question when she'd heard a car in the driveway, slamming doors and teenage boys' voices. So she had run like crazy, leaving the candy bar collection undisturbed, which was probably a good thing. Knowing Nicholas—knowing for instance that he was planning to be a famous detective someday—she had to believe he knew exactly how many bars were in the box, down to the tiniest Tootsie Roll. It had even occurred to her that the reason that sibling collected candy bars was so he could use them as bait to trap chocoholics and other would-be thieves.

She had never risked going back to find out whether Nicholas would know if one of his candy bars disappeared. But, on the other hand, she had never been anywhere near as hungry as she was at that particular minute. She would, she decided, take the risk.

She was backing out of the closet with the first bite of a big Snickers bar already in her mouth when a voice said,

"Well, would you look at that. Looks like I caught me a chocolate thief red-handed."

With the first gulp of Snickers bar caught in her throat, Xandra whirled around to face, not Nicholas, but Quincy. Tall, skinny Quincy, the fish collector, and the oldest and most smart-mouthed of the siblings, who was, at the moment, grinning fiendishly as he moved closer. "Red-handed," he said again, "or maybe in this case, chocolate-fingered might be a better proof of guilt."

Xandra tried for the kind of sneer that would imply that Quincy's wisecrack was, as usual, pretty corny. But a good sneer was hard to manage with a mouth full of chocolate.

"So," Quincy continued, "I guess I'm going to have to decide whether to turn you in or let the Sherlock Holmes of Heritage Avenue make his own deductions."

Xandra chewed and swallowed while she thought hard and fast. Deciding to pick up on the Sherlock Holmes thing, she said, "Yeah, why don't we see if old Nicholas can figure it out?" She tried to echo Quincy's grin as she went on. "I mean, he probably needs the detecting practice."

Quincy stepped back into the doorway and spread his long arms and legs, blocking Xandra's escape route. He was still smiling. "Well, you may be right about that. About Nick needing the practice. Not that many criminal types to practice on here on law-abiding old Heritage Avenue." His grin got more devilish. "But the important question right at this minute is: What should I do about the thief I just caught in the act?" The grin got wider and meaner. "Wouldn't I be encouraging criminal behavior if I let . . ." He paused and then went on. "How did you happen to know about Nick's candy bars, anyway?"

Xandra decided to try the truth or something close to it. "I was just looking around," she said. "I came in here a long time ago to look at his other collections and I just happened to see the candy bars. I didn't take one, though. This is the first one I've taken." Watching Quincy closely, Xandra said, "Why do you think he collects candy bars, anyway? Do you think he just uses them like bait, so he can catch people stealing?"

Quincy chuckled. "Might be part of it. But I think it's mostly because Nelson collects candy bars too. I don't know who started it but they both do it. You know how it is with the Twinsters. Anything one of them does, the other one has to do it faster and higher and bigger and better, or die trying."

Xandra felt confused. A part of it was surprise that she and Quincy were actually having a kind of conversation and that she was learning some things. She'd always had a suspicion that Quincy, who definitely wasn't the contact-sport type, kind of hated it that the twins were such famous jocks. But she hadn't thought about the twins being jealous of each other.

"I didn't know that," she said. "I never knew that they ever tried to beat each other out. I thought they always just liked to gang up on other people. Being twins was probably what did it." She shrugged and raised her eyebrows. "Like, it's always two against one in your favor." Quincy laughed, so she went on, "What did you call them? The Twinsters?"

Quincy nodded. "You got it. Good name for those two, huh? As in, twin gangsters."

Xandra was beginning to feel that she might also be

learning something about Quincy himself. The confused feeling was warming into a kind of curiosity when Quincy's grin returned with a vengeance. "So," he said, "I wonder if people who steal candy bars are also into stealing fish food?"

A sudden stab of fear shot through Xandra—fear for her very private secret—and with the fear came anger. Her throat was tightening and her eyes were blinking fiercely as she said, "What are you talking about? I don't know what you're talking about."

Quincy made a snorting noise. "I'll bet you do," he said. "I'm talking about brine shrimp. I'm talking about a lot of my brine shrimp that just up and disappeared out of the refrigerator a while back."

Xandra tried to push past her oldest, meanest sibling and escape from the room. But his long arms moved to hold her back. "Okay," he said. "You tell me what you did with my brine shrimp and I'll let you go. Okay?"

Suddenly feeling absolutely desperate, Xandra struggled fiercely. Clutching the remains of the Snickers bar in first one fist and then the other, she swung both of them and also kicked as hard as she could. But Quincy hit back. Before she got away, Xandra had been swatted on the backside and slapped on the side of the face, and when she finally made it back to her room, she was teeth-clenchingly, mind-numbingly angry. It took several minutes before she was able to calm down enough to start thinking about anything else. Even about the important question of what had happened to her in the basement less than an hour before. What had happened—and why?

8

XANDRA MUST HAVE eaten the squashed candy bar without really noticing she was doing it, certainly without enjoying it. By the time she could think about anything except how furious she was at Quincy, Nicholas's candy bar had disappeared. Nothing remained except a few chocolate-colored smears on her fingers and around her mouth. The only good news was that the worst of her hunger pangs had vanished along with the candy. It wasn't until then that she could stop concentrating on her stomach—not to mention what she wished she'd done to a certain big bully of a sibling—and turn her thoughts back to something a thousand times more important. Dreadfully, horribly important, but right at the moment, and in that particular place, almost too horrible to be believed.

She was feeling safe now. Safe and sound behind the firmly closed door of her own room. Her own private space with its rain forest mural along one wall, its built-in bookshelves along two others, and above the shelves her huge collection of beautifully framed pictures of enchanted places. Paintings by people with names like Boyle and Bosch and Brueghel, of beautiful half-human creatures, haunted forests, and fairy-tale castles, were everywhere, filling up every bit of empty wall space. And against the far wall, her bed, piled high with her huge collection of stuffed animals. Kicking off her shoes, Xandra climbed onto her bed, pushing her way into the middle of the stack. Now that she was surrounded by her own safe and silent creatures, the weird things that had happened in the basement were beginning to seem more and more unreal.

Digging under the enormous pile of dogs, cats, raccoons and hedgehogs—as well as the yard-long velvet alligator—she picked up her favorite, an almost life-sized skunk. With the soft and cuddly stuffed Stinky draped across her lap, she stroked its long white-striped tail and tried unsuccessfully to blot out the vivid memories that kept rising up behind her eyes. Could all of it, the whole thing, the swelling, bulging clumps of darkness, the flashing eyes and the cruel piercing teeth, have been nothing more than a dream? Not an ordinary, sound-asleep-type dream, she knew that. No normal dream images were ever that sharp and clear and long-lasting. But as she once again ran her hand down over her smooth, unbitten ankles, she began to wonder if it all could have been some extraordinary kind of nightmare.

She could almost believe that was true. But then again,

there was the fact that the incredibly sharp-edged images were still right there in her mind's eye, refusing to fade away as a normal dream always did. Was there such a thing as an enchanted nightmare? Xandra wished she knew, wished there was some way of knowing for sure.

But of course there might be a way. Belinda probably knew—or could find out. Belinda and her grandfather—that must have been who she had meant when she had said that *he* should have warned her about what might happen. So tomorrow, Xandra promised herself, she would find out exactly what Belinda knew. And in the meantime she would find other things to put her mind on. Things like . . . A glance at her watch told her that the first thing she had to put her mind on was getting ready for dinner, and after that . . . After dinner the only alternative to a lonely evening of frightening memories might have to be . . . television.

Xandra had never been crazy about TV because of the Hobson Habitat rule that kids couldn't have televisions in their own rooms. Which meant that a person with so many older and stronger siblings never got to hold the remote and decide what to watch. But on that night, she decided almost anything would be better than watching the nightmare scenes her own mind kept producing when there was nothing to blot them out.

But wouldn't you know it, nearly the whole family was in the family room that night and most of the time nothing at all was happening except a lot of talk. Both the parents were at home by then and all that was going on were conversations about one of two topics—money and Mozart. Actually Mozart came first, because one of the siblings was getting ready to play a Mozart thing at a concert and she was fussing about how hard it was to play and how scared she was. And the rest of the family were all telling her she'd be great and she shouldn't be nervous. Xandra didn't say anything, but what she thought was that some people just pretended to be nervous to get attention. In Xandra's opinion that particular sibling, the fourteen-year-old named Victoria, wasn't ever really nervous or the least bit uncertain about what and who she was, and probably not about what she could or couldn't do either.

And Xandra ought to know. After all, she and Victoria were only two years apart in age, and until Gussie turned up, the only females. Except for Helen, of course, the mother of all of them. But since Helen was a very successful and extremely busy lawyer, she hardly counted as part of the family. There had been a time, back before Gussie was born, that Tory, as Xandra used to call Victoria, had been a little bit better than your average sibling. A certain period when she and Xandra used to have secrets and play games together. But then, as she got older and more perfect on the piano, as well as in a lot of other ways, she got tired of games and of Xandra too. But she obviously wasn't tired of being the center of attention while everybody told her how incredibly talented she was and how she was going to steal the whole show at the recital.

The other topic, the one about money, was started, as usual, by Henry, the father of the Hobson family. Henry was something called a stockbroker, which, as Xandra understood it, meant that he did very important things with money. Things like moving it around the world in complicated, mysterious ways, and making a lot of it that he got to keep for himself. For himself and for his big beautiful family was what he always said. Xandra had heard him say that and a lot of other things about money many times before. So the boring talk about Mozart and money went on and on, but at least boring was better than terrifying.

❧ ❧ ❧

At last the evening and a fairly sleepless night were over and Xandra was on her way to school and to the all-important meeting with Belinda. But if what you had to say was too urgent to wait for the bus ride to the downtown terminal, what then? What then, if it was a sunny morning and lots of people were hanging around in the outdoor lunch area? The only answer was that she would have to find another private place like . . . like the storage room behind the auditorium stage. Which meant she would have to let Belinda know that they absolutely had to talk, in some fairly unnoticeable way, like sliding a note through the crack at the bottom of her locker.

But even after Xandra wrote the message and got it into the locker, Belinda didn't show up. Xandra waited among the old dusty stage sets and costume racks until the first bell rang, wondering and worrying that Belinda might have skipped school that day or perhaps had failed to find the note. And then, after she'd given up and was making her way back down the crowded hall, there she was. There Belinda was, looking perfectly normal—normal for Belinda at least—heading down the hall toward Mr. Fernandez's first-period class.

After glancing quickly around to be sure no one important was watching, Xandra hurried to catch up. When they were side by side, she punched Belinda with her elbow and whispered out of the corner of her mouth, "Didn't you get my note?"

"This note?" Belinda stopped walking and pulled the tightly folded piece of notebook paper out of the pocket of her disgusting jacket. "Yes, I read it."

Reluctantly Xandra stopped too, long enough to inspect the note, which was hers, all right. And then to say in an exasperated tone of voice, "Then why didn't you come? I waited there for a long time."

Belinda looked worried. "I couldn't," she said.

"Why not?" Xandra was getting upset. So furious, in fact, that for a moment she forgot to worry about who might be watching. "What do you mean you couldn't?"

Belinda sighed. "Because I wasn't ready. I didn't get to talk . . ." She paused. "I didn't get to talk to . . ."

"Who?" Xandra demanded. "Who didn't you get to talk to? Your grandfather?"

Belinda shook her head but Xandra noticed that her hands were twisting nervously. "To a person who might know about . . ." Belinda paused.

"Who might know about what?" Xandra insisted.

"About why it happened the way it did." She reached out, grabbed Xandra's arm and shook it. "Don't worry. I'll find out soon. Tonight, I think. And then we'll talk. All right?"

"No," Xandra said. "It's not all right. I want to know right now. Why can't we talk right now?"

Belinda looked around, her worried frown changing to a teasing smile. "Right now? Right here?"

"Well." Xandra looked around too and saw Marcie and

a bunch of her friends heading toward them. "Well, when then?" she asked. "When can we talk?"

"Tomorrow," Belinda said. "Maybe tomorrow after I've found out more about it. All right?"

It wasn't really all right but Xandra shrugged and said it was. Then she stopped to wait for Marcie while Belinda started down the hall. Started, but then suddenly turned and came back. Grabbing Xandra's arm again, she leaned forward to whisper in her ear. "Don't forget your promise not to do anything. Anything with the Key, I mean. It's terribly important."

"Hey, turn loose." Pulling her arm free, Xandra said, "Don't worry. I won't."

As Belinda disappeared into the crowd, Marcie and her Mob of friends caught up and a girl named Katlyn said, "Hey, Alexandra. Who's your new friend?" And at the same time Marcie herself asked, "What was that freak telling you, Alexandra?" Marcie was laughing and so were all the rest of them. That was the way it was with the Mob. Whatever Marcie did, they all did.

Suddenly Xandra was angry at all of them. "Nothing," she said. "Nothing you'd understand." Then she turned her back on the Mob and stomped into the classroom.

EVEN THOUGH THERE was a lot to do at school the rest of that day, the hours crept by slowly. But the last class was finally over, followed by a frustrating bus ride home during which Belinda refused to talk about anything important. And then another long school day had to be lived through before Xandra could hope to get some answers to her questions. Answers to the terribly important questions about what had really happened in the basement, and what had only seemed to be happening, as well as what might happen next.

"Okay, what did you find out?" Xandra started before Belinda had finished stowing her book bag in the overhead rack. "What were those things? And what was going on? I mean, were those awful things real, or did we kind of dream them?"

Belinda stared at Xandra thoughtfully for a long time before she answered. "A dream? Maybe you could call it that." She nodded. "Yes. Maybe that's how you ought to think about it."

Suddenly Xandra was angry. "I don't want to know how I *ought* to think about it. What I want to know is what were they. What were those awful dark blobs full of eyes and teeth?"

Belinda shook her head, her eyes on the ground. "I don't know. That is, I don't know how to explain."

"Why not?" Xandra insisted. "Because you really don't know how or because . . . Or maybe because your grandfather told you not to tell me."

Belinda looked up quickly. For a long moment they stared at each other before Belinda took a deep breath and said, "No. Not exactly. He did tell me it was a mistake to show you how to use the Key. He said I made a mistake to ask him if I could, and he made a mistake too, because you were . . ." Belinda paused and then went on. "Because things were different than what he expected."

"Different?" Xandra interrupted impatiently. "What does that mean?"

There was a long pause. "My grandfather said he thought you—he thought the whole thing would be very different, that's all." Belinda was silent for a moment before she took a deep breath and said, "He said we shouldn't—you shouldn't—use the Key like that anymore. Not ever."

Xandra's frustration was about to boil over when Belinda reached out toward her and said, "Wait. You shouldn't get angry."

"Why not? Why shouldn't I be angry? You and your witch doctor grandfather . . ."

Belinda glanced up, obviously checking to see if anyone had overheard. "Shhh," she pleaded. "Don't say things like that." There was concern, maybe even fright, in her voice and in her dark eyes.

Watching her closely, Xandra asked, "Like what? Like calling your grandfather a witch doctor? Isn't he something like that? He must be."

Belinda shook her head decisively. "No. Nothing like that."

"What is he, then?" Xandra demanded. "If he's not a witch doctor or some kind of wizard, how come he knows about things like my enchanted feather and what would happen to me if I used it?"

"He's just a very wise person. And he wouldn't have told me how to use the Key if I hadn't begged him to. It was my fault. And he didn't expect what happened. Not at all." Belinda turned away and then slowly turned back. She was speaking hesitantly, uncertainly, as she went on. "Maybe it would be better if you asked him about it yourself. If I could take you to see him, would you go? Would you do that?"

A sudden rush of surprise wiped out Xandra's anger and left her feeling shaken and unsure. Shaken at first, but after a bit, curious—eagerly curious.

"Yes," she said. "I *do* want to do that. When? When can I see him?"

Belinda thought for a moment before she asked, "How about tomorrow, Saturday? I could ask him tonight and if it's not all right I'll phone you from the service station and tell you not to come. But probably tomorrow would be good. Could you come then?"

Before Belinda had finished telling her where to go and how to get there, Xandra was nodding confidently. "Don't worry," she said. "I'll be there. The old service station on Greenhill Road, around ten o'clock. I can do that."

When Belinda asked what she would tell her folks about where she was going, she went on to say, "You're not going to tell them you're going to see a wizard, or anything like that, are you?"

Xandra shrugged. "Why would I do that? He's not a wizard, right? You told me he wasn't. And I don't think I'll have to tell anyone much about where I'm going."

"Really?" Belinda seemed doubtful. "You won't need to tell anyone? How will you get money for the bus?"

"I have enough money," Xandra said. "I always have my allowance and I have lots of money saved up. I don't use all of my allowance very often."

Belinda still looked uncertain as they got off the bus, and she had only gone a few steps when she stopped and came back. "Where is it now?" she said, lowering her voice as if there were someone around to hear. "Where do you keep the Key?"

Xandra's hand went to her chest, over the place where the feather hung around her neck on its string. "Right here," she said. "I always have it right here."

"Always?" Belinda asked.

Xandra nodded. "Always."

Reaching out, Belinda took hold of Xandra's arm. "But you won't try to use it by yourself, will you? Something awful might happen if you do."

Xandra shook off Belinda's hand. "No, I won't. I said I wouldn't and I won't. You don't have to keep reminding me."

Belinda turned away again and this time she kept on going. Xandra watched until she was out of sight.

10

XANDRA HAD BEEN right about not having to tell anyone where she was going on Saturday. Saturdays were nearly always golf days for Henry Hobson, and lately for Quincy too, and Helen and Victoria had gone off early to shop for clothes to wear to the big Mozart recital. That left the twins, but not for long. A little later they left too, sounding like a whole herd of horses as they clattered down the back stairs in their baseball shoes. Nobody asked Xandra what she was going to do or where she was going. Nobody except Clara, and that hardly counted. It had been a long time since she and Xandra had paid much attention to each other. So when Clara was getting Gussie ready to go play in the park and asked Xandra to go with them, Xandra laughed and said no thanks. The "no thanks" was polite enough, but the way she laughed said what she really thought of the idea.

It was a dull, gray day as Xandra caught the Heritage Avenue bus that wound its way down the wide street bordered on each side by big houses, tall trees and broad, well-tended lawns. Lawns, however, that at this time of year were turning a dull brown from frostbite in spite of everything gardeners like Otto could do. Closing her eyes to the dreary scene and drearier weather, Xandra concentrated on where she was going and the exciting things she might be able to learn before the day was over. At the downtown terminal she hurried—ran, practically—to the other side of the station, where the No. 70 bus left on its way out into the country and eventually on to the town of Grover.

She would not, however, need to go quite that far. Following Belinda's instructions, she waited until the subdivisions ended and the shopping malls gave way to farmland, and then began to watch for a mileage sign that said GROVER 19 MILES. Just beyond that sign a service station came into view. A small service station under a large weather-beaten sign that said JERRY'S AUTO SHOP. Xandra got off the bus a little uncertainly. It seemed such a strange place for anyone to live, such a long way from residential areas or shopping centers.

Feeling she might have made a mistake, she looked around nervously, but then there she was. There Belinda was, sitting on the bus stop bench just where she'd said she would be, looking a little bit different but not any less weird. Belinda's Saturday outfit was an ancient denim jacket covered with dozens of faded patches, and below that, a ragged pair of blue jeans, and her long straggly hair was pulled back into a loose braid. When she saw Xandra, her smile came and went quickly, and so did what she had to say.

"All right. Let's go," was all she said before she led the way down a narrow country road. When Xandra asked how far it was, she only said, "Not very. Come on. Let's hurry." They went on walking, passing a dumping yard for dead cars, two or three run-down houses and then some open fields. The tiny, deserted houses and the wide empty stretches of land made Xandra feel uneasy. She didn't know why, except that having grown up behind high walls and fences made the endless emptiness seem strangely threatening. Finally, when Belinda turned off the road onto a narrow lane between tall trees, Xandra stopped dead and demanded, "You didn't tell me we had to go way out into the country. I mean, where are we actually going?"

Belinda's answer, when it came, seemed to be to a different question. "I think it will be all right," she said. "He doesn't always talk to new people but when I asked him he said he wanted to meet you."

"Wait a minute," Xandra said. "You only *think* it will be all right? Why didn't you tell me your grandfather doesn't like to meet new people?" Grabbing Belinda's sleeve, she pulled her to a stop. "What if he decides he doesn't want to see me? What will he do?"

Belinda shook her head. "He won't do anything. Sometimes he just won't talk. Even to people who have come a long way to see him. But he said he wanted you to come. He said he needed to find out . . ."

She paused then and interrupted herself, abruptly changing the subject. Pointing down the road, she said, "There. See that gate up there on the left? That's where we turn off."

A few yards farther on, a sagging wooden gate opened

onto an overgrown dirt road that led up a slope toward what seemed to be . . . a farm perhaps? Or perhaps only the remains of something that had once been a farm. The house came first. Halfway up the hill, almost hidden among tall trees, it was a tall narrow structure whose peeling paint, dangling shutters and weed-grown yard gave it a sad, deserted, almost haunted look. And beyond the house the lopsided, sagging roof of an old barn soon came into view.

The possibility that Belinda's grandfather was a farmer was, for some reason, a little bit reassuring. Xandra didn't know why, except that you don't often hear of farmers who are also wizards or witch doctors. Xandra was about to ask Belinda if she and her family were farmers when she saw something that seemed to answer the question. An old man dressed in overalls and carrying a large pail was coming out of the barn and heading toward the house. A huge old man whose bearded face sagged into droopy wrinkles and whose long grayish hair was tied into a ponytail. When he saw Belinda and Xandra, he stopped and waited for them. His eyes, almost hidden under the bushy eyebrows, were small and fierce. He was not smiling.

"Now who's this?" he growled, looking from Xandra to Belinda.

"Just a friend of mine," Belinda said quickly. "She's not here to . . . She's just here to see me."

Xandra turned to stare angrily at Belinda. She was about to protest. To say, No, I came to ask you some important questions, when Belinda grabbed her arm and pulled her away.

"Hey," Xandra said as she let herself be led toward the

barn. "I thought you said he was going to talk to me. To explain about—"

"Shhh," Belinda interrupted. "That's not my grandfather. That's just Ezra."

When Xandra looked back, the decrepit man named Ezra had turned away and, still carrying the pail, was heading toward the equally decrepit house. "Ezra?" she asked. "Who's Ezra?"

Tugging Xandra along after her, Belinda didn't answer until they had reached the far edge of the barnyard. It was there they stopped to watch the old man climb some rickety stairs and disappear into the house.

"Does he actually live there, in that haunted house?" Xandra asked.

Belinda nodded. "Ezra has lived right there in that same old house all his life, I guess. My grandfather has known him practically forever. A long time ago my grandfather lived here in the commune. So last summer when we had to get out of . . ." She paused and began again. "When we needed to move, Ezra said he could come here again, at least for a while." Belinda turned and pointed down a sloping dirt road that led to a large grove of trees. "Down there where the commune used to be."

"The commune?" Xandra asked.

"Yes, you know. When a lot of people kind of live and work together," Belinda said. But Xandra didn't know, so Belinda went on to tell about how it had been a popular thing to do for a while, for people to move out to the country and live together in large groups that were sometimes called communes. "There was a famous commune right here on Ezra's farm," she said. "Some people called it Ezra's Eden. It was a big one, almost a hundred people sometimes, and my grandfather was part of it for a while. So when we needed a place to live, Ezra let him come back."

"One hundred people?" Xandra was incredulous. "Right down there?"

Belinda nodded. "Come on. You'll see."

They went on down a steep slope, and as they entered the grove of trees, Xandra noticed two tiny, roughly built houses and then a slightly larger one. Only three un-painted, run-down cabins, each one with cement block steps leading up to a rickety front porch. A thin plume of smoke was rising from the chimney of the larger house, but that was the only sign of life. "One hundred people?" Xandra asked again, not believing it for a minute.

"For a while there were," Belinda said, "a long time ago. There were a lot more houses then. And tents too. Some of the people lived in tents."

"And who lives here now?" Xandra asked. "Besides you and your grandfather."

Belinda shook her head. "No one else," she said. "Just us. We live mostly in that biggest house but we can use the others too."

Xandra checked out the three cabins. They all looked pretty shabby and dilapidated and so small that even the biggest would probably fit into the Hobson family room.

As if she were reading Xandra's mind, Belinda said, "I know. They're nothing much, but they do have electricity and the big one has a kitchen and real bathroom."

"A kitchen?" An interesting thought came to mind. "Who does the cooking? Your grandfather?"

Belinda shook her head, smiling. "Not much. Sometimes we eat at Ezra's, and I can cook a little."

"Wow." Xandra was impressed. "I can make sandwiches but that's about it." A related question occurred to her. "And how about the rest of it? Like shopping and house-cleaning. Do you do that too?"

Belinda shrugged. "Ezra shops but I do most of the housework. Sweeping mostly. There used to be a vacuum cleaner but it broke." She looked around for a minute, and then, sounding surprised almost, as if she'd never noticed before, she said, "I guess it does look pretty trashy, but I do have my own house and that's the best part." She pointed toward the nearest cabin, a tiny shack with lots of missing shingles and a broken window. "This one is mine. I keep all my own things in it. You want to see?"

Xandra shrugged. "Sure," she said. "Why not?"

A screen door, and then a creaking wooden one, led into a room that had, to Xandra's surprise, a strangely familiar feel. Like her own room in the Hobson Habitat, it was full of books and pictures. Lots of books sat on long shelves made of bricks and planks, or were arranged in neat stacks near an ancient saggy couch. And, most amazing, the walls were covered with pictures, and some of them were the same kinds of pictures Xandra had been collecting all her life. Pictures of beautiful forests where trees had living faces, of strangely beautiful creatures half animal and half human and of people who were obviously characters from fantastic fairy-tale worlds. Walking around the room staring at the pictures and reading the titles of the books, most of which she had read too, Xandra was beginning to feel almost at home.

"Hey," she said. "I like it. And it's all just yours? Nobody else's?"

Belinda nodded.

"Great," Xandra said. She looked around. "Does it have other rooms?"

Belinda nodded again. There was one other room in the cabin but it seemed to be nothing more than a storage area. A whole room crammed full of huge cardboard boxes, all of which were full to overflowing with articles of clothing. Very old clothing.

"Wow," Xandra said. "Where did you get all . . ."

"It's from the commune," Belinda said. "When people went off and left some of their clothing, Ezra always saved it in case they came back for it. But most of them never came back, so now it's mine. Ezra gave all of it to me."

As Xandra watched Belinda shake out a long, flowery skirt and then a badly faded tie-dyed T-shirt, she was intrigued for more reasons than one. Intrigued at first because she was remembering the games she and Tory used to play, which involved dressing up in old stuff they found in boxes and trunks in the Hobsons' attic. She became even more interested when she suddenly realized she was looking at the source of Belinda's weird school outfits. But all she said was, "There sure is a lot of it."

"I know." Belinda looked pleased. She was carefully folding away the ragged skirt when a sudden sound made her hurry to the cabin's door. Motioning for Xandra to join her, she whispered, "Here he is now. Here's my grandfather."

11

AT FIRST GLANCE the man who was standing in the doorway of the largest cabin was almost a disappointment. Xandra wasn't sure what she had been expecting, but it did seem that a wizard or even a person who knew about such things as dangerous enchanted gifts ought to look at least a little bit weird. But the man who was standing on the steps of the large cabin was, at first glance, fairly ordinary-looking.

Checking him out carefully as she and Belinda walked toward him, Xandra noticed that he was tall and rather thin, and dressed in a dark sweatshirt and trousers. His hair was gray and his long narrow face didn't look especially old or young. His eyes were not especially scary or threatening, Xandra decided—except that when they looked at you, it was hard to look away and even harder to remember what you meant to say and exactly how you were planning to say it.

"Hello, Alexandra. I've been expecting you." The voice went with the eyes, deep and steady. He nodded to Belinda and gestured toward a row of chairs at one end of the front porch. "Belinda, child. Bring our guest up here."

While they were climbing the steps and finding places to sit, Belinda beside Xandra, and the grandfather facing them, his eyes were turned elsewhere, and Xandra found that she was able to feel more herself. More the frankly outspoken or even, as some people put it, smart-mouthed Xandra Hobson. Trying for her usual supercool smile, she began, "So okay. I'm Xandra, and I guess you're Belinda's grandfather. So should I call you . . . " She had meant to ask if she should call him Grandpa, but when his eyes met hers again, she was suddenly tongue-tied.

Hushed and silent, she found herself concentrating on what he was saying, feeling in some mysterious way that every word had many important, maybe even secret, meanings. "Tell me about yourself, Alexandra." He spoke very softly but in a way that made it impossible not to listen closely and think carefully about what he was asking. "What can you tell me about Alexandra Hobson?"

It was the "Alexandra" that did it. That gave her the push toward another last-ditch effort to be herself. To say something like "Well, in the first place don't call me Alexandra. I hate being Alexandra. And as for being a Hobson, that's even worse." But instead she found herself playing it straight, saying, "About Alexandra Hobson? Yes, my real name is Alexandra but I call myself Xandra and I am part of the Hobson family. You've probably heard about the Hobsons?"

He shook his head, smiling, making fun of her question maybe, even though it was a perfectly sensible one. After all, lots of people *had* heard of the Hobsons. "I've heard a bit from Belinda," he said. "She tells me you come from a large family?"

Xandra tried for her usual disgusted grimace and her favorite sarcastic comment about having lost count of how many siblings she had. But the familiar words were somehow out of reach. She nodded. "Yes, a large family," she mumbled, and then, hanging her head to escape the dark, overpowering eyes, "I guess I don't want to talk about it." She breathed deeply, clenching her fists, feeling confused and angry, resentful of whatever was keeping her from making her usual sharp-edged comments. Still looking down at her hands, she asked, "Why do you want to know about me? I thought I was going to get to ask you questions."

The grandfather's deep voice seemed to echo through her head as he said, "Soon. That will be soon. But before I can answer your questions correctly I must know more about you. About you and your family and the people and things that are important to you."

Xandra didn't get it. Why would knowing about her and her family explain the vicious, sharp-fanged creatures that had appeared out of nowhere in her familiar basement hideout? She took a deep breath and tried again to resist. "Tell you about me and my family?" She said the exact words she'd intended to, but they didn't come out the way she'd expected. She'd meant it to sound surprised and sarcastic. Like, "Tell *you* about *me* and my family? Why should I do a thing like that?" But instead, with her eyes caught again by his, she only repeated the question and then began to answer it.

"Well, there are my parents. My father is Henry Hobson, the stockbroker, but my mother is the really famous one. She's Helen Hobson." She gave him a chance to say, "Oh, you mean *the* Helen Hobson?" But he didn't, so she went on. "Well, she's this very important lawyer and she's handled a lot of famous cases. And then there are five kids." She paused, narrowed her eyes and added, "Six, if you want to count me."

She was expecting him to ask what most people would have: "Why shouldn't I count you?"

But he didn't, at least not quite. Instead he only nodded slowly and said, "And why do you think you don't count?"

This time her determination to avoid giving a straight answer was even less strong and certain. Instead, after only a second's hesitation, she began, "Well, all of them, all the other Hobsons, are really great at something. At everything, actually. Not just at school but at things like . . . Well, there's Quincy, for instance, he's the oldest and he's this incredible scientist. Like he's won so many prizes that all the science fairs started giving out two blue ribbons—one for Quincy Hobson and the other for whoever happens to come in second. And the twins are next. They're good at school too, especially math, but mostly they're practically famous athletes, both of them. And really good-looking. All the girls in six school districts are completely gaga about them. The twins are sixteen and Victoria, the next one, is fourteen. She's not just good, she's perfect. At everything, especially playing the piano. I came next and I guess after they saw me they decided I would be the last one. And I *was* for almost seven years. But then they had Gussie. Augusta Katherine, that is. And Gussie is . . . Well, according to Clara, Gussie is the most beautiful thing God ever created. She says so all the time."

"Clara?" the deep voice asked.

Xandra meant to simply shrug and say, "Oh, Clara isn't part of the family. She's just a kind of full-time baby-sitter." But somehow she found herself saying, "She's a nurse who's been living at our house most of the time since . . . well, since I was born, at least." She swallowed against a tightness in her throat. "Yeah, since right after I was born and my mother went back to work and opened her own office." She grinned, and repeating an old family joke, she said, "There's a family joke that I thought Clara was my mother until I was six years old."

"I see," the grandfather said. "Yes, I see." And then for what seemed like a long time he didn't say anything more. Instead he just sat there staring at Xandra, making her feel more and more uncomfortable and impatient.

She looked down at her feet, protecting her eyes from the old man's magnetic stare, and took a deep breath. "Okay," she said. "Isn't that enough? Is it my turn now?" No answer. She looked up and said it again more loudly and insistently. "When is it going to be my turn to ask some questions?"

At last he nodded. "Yes," he said. "You wanted to ask what it was that attacked you in the basement of your home?"

"Yeah, that's it," Xandra said. "That's what I thought I was coming here to find out about. What those things were and where they came from. They weren't just a dream, were they? Like some special kind of nightmare that goes on seeming absolutely real even after it's all over?"

He shook his head. "No, not a dream."

"Then what were they? Are you going to tell me or not?"

The grandfather's eyes caught and held hers again and he spoke slowly and distinctly.

"The creatures that appeared to you have been called many things by those of us who . . ." He paused and began again. "People who have been aware of them have given them many names. Some have known them only as shadows, or shades or even chimeras, but at other times they have been called *reflejos* or *spiegels*. I myself have called them unseen entities, or simply the Unseen."

"The Unseen," Xandra repeated. "What does that mean?" There was no answer. The grandfather had gone back to staring at Xandra as if she were some kind of scientific exhibit. She turned to Belinda and demanded, "Do you know what he's talking about?"

Belinda nodded. "Yes, I think so. He'll tell you if you listen. Just listen and don't . . ."

"Don't what?"

Belinda's voice had sunk to a whisper. "Don't get angry."

"Why not? Why shouldn't I get angry?"

"Because that's what makes it so dangerous for . . ." Glancing at her grandfather, Belinda stopped in midsentence. And then went on, "He'll tell you why it happened the way it did."

"All right. Tell me. Where did those horrible things come from? I mean, they must have come from somewhere, because they were never there in the basement before. I know that. I mean, the basement, at least the part that's back behind the furnace, is my own special place. I've been there a million times. So I want to know where those things came from, and why." A disturbing thought intruded. "Was it the Key? Was it the Key that brought them?"

"No, it didn't bring them. And they didn't come from anywhere. They were just there. They're just there—everywhere—all the time."

Xandra stared at Belinda. "No," she said. "You're lying. If they're all around us all the time, why don't we know about them? Why can't we see them or hear them, or feel them like I felt those things in the basement?"

Belinda glanced at the grandfather, who nodded as if telling her to go on. "People can't see them or hear them because they don't have the right kind of senses. You know, senses, like seeing and hearing and feeling and smelling. But that doesn't mean they aren't there."

Beginning to get it, to understand what Belinda meant, Xandra gasped. "You mean that's what happened with the feather when you . . ." Pretending to hold something in her hands, she pressed them to her forehead the way Belinda had done with the feather. And as she did, she remembered very clearly the strange sensations she had felt, as if her eyes and ears and even her skin were stretching and growing. "You mean I changed my senses when I did that with the feather?"

Belinda nodded, and when Xandra turned to the grand-father, he nodded too. Xandra was quiet then, thinking and wondering, thinking of something entirely unaccept-able. Something that just couldn't be true. Finally she burst out, "Do you mean that they couldn't have bitten me if I hadn't used the Key?"

Belinda was starting to answer, slowly and uncertainly, when the grandfather interrupted. "Yes," he said. "Without the use of the Key you wouldn't have been able to experi-ence the Unseen in the way that you did."

Xandra's mind was spinning, turning into a whirlpool of disappointment and then anger. She had been so sure that the feather was some sort of wonderful magical gift given to her by an enchanted creature as a reward for sav-ing its life. "What's the good of it, then? What's the good of having a magical gift if it just lets a bunch of monsters chew on you?"

"Such creatures of the Unseen can have many forms, I'm afraid. Their shapes can change constantly. Some peo-ple find them to be harmless, even comforting, as I thought they might be for you. Or, as you discovered, they can be violent and painful." The grandfather paused and his lips twitched on the edge of a smile. "Or there can be situations in which they can, as you say, chew on one."

If he was making a joke of it, Xandra didn't think it was funny. "Well, I just don't believe it. Any of it. I don't believe there are these evil . . ." She stopped, trying to remember. "These evil, whatever you called them . . ."

"Creatures of the Unseen," Belinda whispered.

"You mean these evil creatures are all around, all the time? I don't know why you're lying to me, but you are."

Xandra jumped to her feet. "I'm going now. I'm leaving and you better not try to stop me."

As she started to move toward the stairs that led down from the porch, the grandfather's eyes met hers and she felt quieted and stilled, but only for a moment. "We won't stop you," he was saying, "but I do think you had better leave your Key here." He put out his hand, and for a moment Xandra's hand went to the string around her neck.

"Why?" she whispered. "It's mine."

"Yes, it is yours," he said, "but no one owns a Key for long. It is a power that is given rarely and then only briefly, and its use can be dangerous. It is possible to find oneself lost in the Unseen."

But Xandra didn't want to hear. Forcing her eyes away from his quiet stare, she shouted, "No. You can't have it." She turned and ran, ran down the steps and went on running out of the grove, up the hill, past the ghostly farmhouse and out onto the lonely country road. She stopped then and looked back to see if anyone was following her, but no one was. Not even Belinda.

12

THE TWO BUS rides, the long one into town and then the shorter one on the Heritage Avenue Express, lasted so long that by the time Xandra got home, lunch was over and done with and put away. Everything was wrapped and packaged and stored away by Geraldine in one of her king-sized refrigerators, and she said, "I'm not about to get it all out again. If your mother wants me to do lunches she'd better tell you kids to quit thinking you can come in to eat whenever you feel like it." Geraldine, the Hobsons' part-time cook and full-time grouch, usually did dinners only. Except sometimes on weekends when she did lunches, but not without a lot of complaining.

"Okay. Okay," Xandra said. "I'll do it myself. Anybody can make a sandwich." So she did, making herself a big ham and cheese sandwich while Geraldine stood over her complaining about the messy way she wrapped up the left-overs and put things away on the wrong shelves of the refrigerator.

"No, no, not there. In the cheese drawer. And do be careful. You're going to drop that plate," Geraldine was saying while Xandra, on the way across the kitchen, bent over to scratch her leg. Geraldine was still griping when Xandra left the room, slamming the door behind her. In the upstairs hall she ran into Clara, who was heading for the laundry room carrying one of Gussie's frilly doll-baby dresses.

"There you are." Clara's round eyes crinkled into a smile. "I was just looking for you. Have you decided what you're going to wear tonight?"

"Wear? Tonight?" Xandra asked.

She had forgotten for a moment, which under the circumstances wasn't too surprising. After all, she'd had a lot more important things to think about. But then, even after she remembered that the whole family was going to have dinner at some big-deal restaurant before Victoria's recital, she went on pretending she didn't know.

"Wear? Wear where?"

"To Victoria's recital," Clara said. "And to that nice new restaurant on Convention Row." She held up the frilly dress. "I'm on my way to iron this for Gussie and I was just wondering if you might need to have something pressed."

Xandra shook her head and went on down the hall. In her own room she ate her sandwich before she curled up on her bed in the midst of all her animals and started to go over, and over again, the things she'd been told by the grandfather and Belinda. Could any of it be true? Could the feather, the Key, that is, really change your senses so that you could see and feel things that were invisible otherwise? Things that were invisible but always there, all around you but always Unseen, unless you had an enchanted Key.

And what did the grandfather mean when he said a person could be lost in the Unseen? Did he mean that there could be a time when the Key could take you to the Unseen and then leave you trapped there forever? And how could you be sure whether you were completely and finally back in the real world?

It was a frightening thought. Sitting up, clutching her stuffed Stinky and some of her other larger stuffed animals against her chest like a protective shield, she peered over them into every corner of the room. There was, of course, nothing there.

Nothing except what she could almost see, or else imagine seeing, when she squinted and glanced quickly from one side of the room to the other. Was there a sudden, shifting shadow near the baseboard under the far end of the mural, or just behind the edge of the bookcase? She wasn't sure, and as she went on squinting and glancing, she felt less and less sure. Less sure she wasn't seeing something—or perhaps feeling something—weird. Like the way her ankles kept itching, for instance. Her ankles and other places up and down her legs where she'd been bitten by the monsters. At last she flopped back down, and pulling an armful of animals up over her head and face, she whispered over and over again, "It's all a lie. All of it. It's all just a lie." And then someone was shaking her shoulder and she was waking up, and her legs were itching again.

"Xandra," Clara was saying. "Wake up. The taxi will be here in twenty minutes and you have to get ready." And twenty minutes later Xandra, in an only slightly wrinkled linen dress, and Gussie, looking even more than ever like an expensive windup doll, were being put into a taxi and sent off to the fancy new restaurant across the street from the Civic Auditorium.

In the New Age Grill Helen was at the head of the table, of course. All by herself at the moment, since Henry had a late meeting and would have to join them later. To look at her, at her sensible hairdo and business suit, you might think she didn't look very momlike. But when Gussie ran to her skipping and jumping and yelling "Hi, Mommy," all the people in the restaurant, including the waiters, got that sappy "isn't that too cute" look on their faces. Xandra sat down quickly and buried her nose in the menu.

Quincy, who was sitting next to Xandra, seemed uncomfortable in a sport coat and tie and smelled slightly sulfurous, as he often did after an afternoon in the science lab. He grinned at Xandra when she sat down, but she didn't grin back.

The twins were across the table, Greek-god handsome and major-league cool as usual, and next to them was Victoria, the guest of honor, looking supersophisticated in her new evening dress. But not so sophisticated that someone who knew her as well as Xandra did, or as well as Xandra used to before Victoria became so perfect, wouldn't notice that her face was pale and her smile looked a little stiff. Leaning forward, Xandra whispered, "Hey, Tory. Do you remember that time we dressed up in ragbag stuff and pretended we were the Lost Boys?"

Tory stared at Xandra zombielike for a second before she started a shaky smile. "Yes, I remember. The Ragbag Game. Whatever reminded you of that?" Her smile became a little less shaky as she looked down at her new dress and said, "I hope it wasn't this dress?"

Xandra couldn't help giggling. "No, it wasn't your dress that reminded me. I just saw something today that made me remember the ragbag thing." The rest of the family were watching. Watching and smiling approvingly as if they were glad that someone had been able to make Victoria loosen up a little. Turning her face away, Xandra reached down to scratch her ankle before she realized it had stopped itching. At least for the moment.

The recital was a bore, of course, but maybe not quite as much of a bore as Xandra had been expecting. All the soloists were, like Victoria, people who had just won awards at a young musicians' contest, and most of them looked scared to death. Xandra got a little bit interested in imagining what they must have been feeling when they walked onstage and saw all those people staring at them. She was pretty good at that kind of imagining and she really got into the feel of it when Tory came onstage.

And then it was all over and all the Hobsons were back at home and Xandra was back in her own room, curled up in bed under a pile of her animals, and once again thinking about the things the grandfather and Belinda had told her. Thinking and feeing terribly impatient that there would be another whole day before she could see Belinda at school and ask her for more and better explanations and answers. Better answers to the questions she'd already asked, and new answers to some questions that had recently come to mind.

◉ ◉ ◉

Monday morning finally arrived and Xandra, who had caught an early bus, was sitting on the front steps of the school anxiously waiting for Belinda to show up. And then there she was walking up the sidewalk, wearing the same ratty old jacket with its rolled up sleeves and raveled-out lining. Xandra jumped to her feet and ran to meet her.

"Well, at last," Xandra said. "Was your bus late or something?"

"No, I don't think so." Belinda's surprised expression changed to a worried frown. "Why? What's happened?"

Xandra shook her head. "Nothing. At least not about . . ." Looking around, she lowered her voice. "Nothing about the Key, anyway. I didn't try to use it. But there are a bunch of things I need to know about."

"What kind of things?" Belinda stopped walking and seemed to pull away. "I thought we . . . That is, I thought all your questions got answered."

"Not all of them." Xandra looked around. They were partway up the steps to the front entrance of the school, and arriving students were everywhere. "Come on. Let's go over there. Under the tree." Grabbing Belinda's arm, she pulled her away from the crowd and across the lawn. When they were safely out of earshot, if not out of sight, she jerked Belinda to a stop.

Belinda looked nervous and uneasy. "I don't know what

to tell you," she began, and then, "Look. Look over there." Looking in the direction Belinda was pointing, Xandra saw Marcie and a couple of her friends getting out of a big black Cadillac and starting across the street toward the school. "Maybe you want to go see your friends," Belinda suggested. "We could talk later."

Xandra shrugged impatiently. "No," she said. "I don't want to see them. What I want is for you to tell me why your grandfather showed you how to use the Key. Why would he want to do a thing like that? Didn't he know what would happen to you? To me, I mean."

"No, he didn't," Belinda said, "and it was my fault. I didn't tell him enough about you. I just told him how old you are, and how you happened to get the Key, and all the things you said about animals, and how you used to take care of so many of them. Because of what I told him, he didn't think the Unseen would be like it was for you." She paused and then went on. "You remember how it was at first. When we were back there behind the furnace where you kept all your animals? Remember the one you said was like your skunk?"

Xandra couldn't help smiling. "Yeah. And smelled like him too."

"I guess Grandfather thought there would be more things like that. Friendly things."

"Then why weren't there?" Xandra was feeling frustrated again. "Why were some of them monsters?"

Belinda stared down at her feet and then turned toward the steps, where lots of students were still milling around. It was as if she was hoping someone would come to her rescue by interrupting the conversation.

"Well, why wasn't it?" Xandra persisted. "Why wasn't it like your grandfather expected?"

At last Belinda took a deep breath and raised her eyes. "All right," she said, "I'll tell you. Remember when Grandfather told you the creatures were sometimes called *reflejos* or *spiegels*?"

"Yeah, I guess so," Xandra said.

"Well, those are words that mean reflections or mirrors. Like my grandfather told you, those creatures are everywhere, all the time, but they're like an invisible stream of energy that can take on different shapes and forms. And not always the same ones. Mirrors reflect whatever is around them. And if a person has a Key, the Unseen reflects . . ." She paused and then went on, "It reflects things about that person."

Xandra stared at Belinda. At last, narrow-eyed, she began to say, "What you mean is . . ." Long pause. "You mean that those monsters came from me? Were a reflection of me?"

Belinda shook her head. "No, not you. Just something about the way you are made them be the way they were."

"Oh yeah?" Xandra was angry now, and getting angrier. "Well, I don't believe you. Or your weird grandfather either. I mean, I may not be as gorgeous as some people, but those ugly things . . ." Whirling around, she ran across the lawn, and went on running.

13

XANDRA DIDN'T BELIEVE what Belinda had said about mirrors and reflections.

She went on telling herself how much she didn't believe it as she hurried across the lawn and up the front steps of the school. She didn't believe it for one minute, and she was just going to forget all about it. And when she caught up with Marcie and her pals, she really did put it right out of her mind—or thought she did.

For once, in spite of having just seen her talking to Belinda again, most of the Mob were pretty friendly. At least they were after Lisa started sneering about seeing Xandra visiting with her "special friend," and Xandra shut her up by saying, "Yeah, I was talking to Belinda and you'll never guess all the things she was telling me about you."

That really got Lisa's attention. "About me? What sort of things about me?"

Xandra shrugged and said, "Oh, a lot of personal stuff. She has these special powers. Ways to find out about other people's secrets."

The whole bunch of them, all the girls in Marcie's group, were listening now, leaning close in a tight circle, asking questions and begging her to tell them more. So she did. More stuff about how Belinda had a grandfather who was a kind of wizard who was teaching her how to work all kinds of magic spells and find out things about everyone she met. She was still talking when they got to language arts class.

The hours went by quickly that day, with lots to think over as well as talk about. But Xandra was not having any more talks with Belinda. Feeling that she'd heard enough about ugly monsters who were like mirrors, Xandra made it a point to catch the early bus that went directly to Heritage Avenue. And then she was home again, back at the Hobson Habitat, and there she did have a rather unusual talk, but not of course with Belinda.

She was walking down the front hall on her way to the stairs when it happened. As she walked past the door to what was sometimes called the music room, she was hearing but not really listening to what sounded like a rerun of "the perfect one's" recital. But as she passed the door, the music stopped and someone called her name.

"Hey, Xandra," Victoria was calling. "Come in here. I want to talk to you."

Xandra was surprised. It wasn't very often that any of

the siblings wanted to talk to her enough to stop whatever they were doing. Particularly not if it was something as important as Mozart.

"Yeah?" she said, sticking her head in the door. "You want to talk to me right now? You look pretty busy."

Victoria got up from the piano bench. "Not really," she said, shrugging. "I'm just going over the mistakes I made."

"Mistakes? I didn't hear any mistakes." She considered going on to say, I didn't think you ever made a mistake, but decided against it.

"Really?" Victoria looked pleased and hopeful. "That's good. I thought everyone heard them."

Shaking her head, Xandra said, "I'll bet no one heard any mistakes except you and maybe Mr. Randolph." Mr. Randolph was the piano teacher who had started all the Hobson siblings on the piano and given up quickly on most of them. Especially quickly on Xandra.

Victoria sat down on the music room couch and patted the place beside her. "I hope you're right. Come on in here. I want to talk to you."

"About what, for instance?" Reminding herself that it was usually bad news when any of the siblings wanted to talk to her, Xandra was expecting the worst as she stopped just inside the door. But it turned out that all Victoria wanted to talk about was the dressing-up game she and Xandra used to play. The game that Xandra had reminded her of the night before in the restaurant.

"We called it playing the Ragbag Game, didn't we?" Tory said. "I'd sort of forgotten about it but I really remembered when you mentioned it. I wonder if all those ragbags are still there."

"Probably," Xandra said. "Who knows." There had been an awful lot of ragbags in the attic of the Habitat. Some of them were full of things that Clara saved for housecleaning or silver polishing, but some others held great stuff like Helen's old furs and formals and even some things left over from Halloweens and fancy costume parties.

"Do you remember the time we made up a crazy play and I was Cleopatra and you were Tarzan?" Tory said, beginning to giggle. "And my Egyptian wig kept sliding down over my eyes just when I was supposed to do one of my speeches?"

"Yeah, I remember." Xandra tried and failed to hold back a smile. "Yeah, and I kept losing my loincloth." They went on remembering things and Tory went on giggling until Quincy went past the door. When he peeked in to see what all the laughing was about, Tory jumped up and ran to ask him something about what you had to do to get into the driver education class. Xandra started to leave, thinking, "Well, so much for the good old Ragbag days." But before she turned the corner, Tory called after her, "Let's talk about it some more later. Okay, Xandra?"

Back in her own room, Xandra didn't get back to thinking about Belinda and the mirror thing right away, and when she did she was surer than ever that it wasn't true. None of those crazy lies about how the monsters reflected things about the person who owned the Key could possibly be true.

And that stuff about the Unseen creatures being everywhere, all the time. That was even more ridiculous. Suddenly remembering how she had imagined seeing, or maybe really did see, some shadowy shapes right there in her own room, she quickly climbed up on her bed and dug her way down into the bottom of her pile of animals. Clutching some of her favorites against her chest, she squinted and began once again to glance quickly from side to side.

But this time nothing happened, at least not at first. No dark shapes lurked at the edges of bookcases or in the corners of the room. She tried it again, squinting even more, but still no cloudy shapes or flickering shadows. But then, as she was cuddling down into a more comfortable position, rearranging dogs and teddy bears, a dolphin, two plush tigers and then a plaid elephant, she suddenly felt something strange. A squirming, snuggling movement, near her right arm at first, and then against her left leg. A shifting snuggle and then a warm, damp, breathy touch on her wrist. Warm and damp and friendly like the nose of a kitten, or perhaps of a baby skunk. Even though Xandra quickly dug down through all the animals, running her hands over one muzzle after another, she couldn't find a single one that felt the least bit warm or damp.

So perhaps that was the end of it. And if it was, maybe the enchanted feather was a gift after all, instead of an evil charm that created a swarm of flesh-eating monsters. What if the appearance of the sharp-fanged creatures had only been some kind of mistake that would never happen again?

Pulling the feather out from under her blouse, Xandra turned it from side to side, thinking about how at first she had imagined it to be a wonderful thank-you gift from the enchanted bird she had rescued from the hunters and their dog. A gift like an Aladdin's lamp that would grant wonderful wishes and answer all kinds of secret questions. While she was still lying there among her animal buddies, Xandra found she was beginning to think about other magical possibilities that might begin with . . . Perhaps with another visit to the basement? To the secret place behind the furnace where all her animals had lived and where she had first seen the enchanted feather.

∂ ∂ ∂

During the next few days Xandra continued to think about the things that had happened in the basement. Mostly about what had happened after she had used the Key, but before the sinister clumps of darkness began to appear. She thought particularly about the fuzzy little shape that had looked and acted a lot like Stinky. Would he come back again if she went back to her basement hideout? As time went by she became more and more sure that some of her other basement orphans might turn up again if she was brave enough to go looking for them.

She didn't, however, do anything right away. At home and at school she went on doing ordinary things, which, as usual, included a lot of reading and daydreaming. And although she did see Belinda every day, she didn't make any special effort to talk to her. After the day Belinda had told her that the monsters were her own reflection, Xandra had quit riding the downtown bus. Belinda, she told herself, must have wanted it that way since she didn't even bother to ask Xandra why she'd stopped riding with her. So that was it, and everyone seemed to be happy, except that once in a while Xandra found herself thinking of something she'd like to say about a book or an idea, the kind of thing she wouldn't be able to discuss with most of the people she knew. At those times she wished that—that things could be different.

And every evening, back in her own room, Xandra climbed onto her bed and snuggled down among her animals and waited to see if anything would happen. But nothing did. So that's that, she told herself. It's all over. But the truth was, she didn't want to believe it. To believe that the whole enchanted feather thing was over, or else that it had never really happened in the first place.

It wasn't until Saturday morning that she finally made up her mind to go back to her basement hideout in spite of what had happened, or what she thought had happened, the last time she was there. "Just to look around," she whispered, imagining that she was talking to Belinda. "I won't try to use the Key. I just want to go back to where I took care of the animals. What would be wrong with that?"

So it was that early on a Saturday morning, while most of the Hobsons were still asleep, Xandra crept down the back stairs and around the house until she came to the steps that led down to the basement. On the bottom stair she stopped for a moment, for one last aboveground, daylight moment, before she took a deep breath and opened the door.

14

INSIDE THE BASEMENT everything looked pretty much the same as ever. Even in the dim light it was possible to see that the boxes, trunks and barrels were right where they'd always been, as well as all the stacks of bicycles, skateboards, scooters and vacuum cleaners. Taking one careful step at a time, Xandra moved forward, stopping again and again to check all the dark corners and crevices behind the boxes and between the stacks. Crevices where the dusty light barely penetrated, and where, if she looked too long and hard, she could imagine thickening pools of darkness. But where, if she shook her head hard and blinked, there seemed to be only normal shadows. Shaking and blinking every few steps, Xandra moved toward the furnace and around behind it to her own secret hideout.

There too everything was just as it always had been. A

faint animal odor, warm and musty, still hung heavy in the air. And by the dim light that barely filtered in through the high narrow windows, it was possible to see as far as where the old kibble cabinet leaned back against the wall. And on past that to the double row of boxes and cages that had held so many animals and birds.

And only a few feet farther on was the padded box where she'd put the wounded bird, and where, early the next morning, she had found the enchanted feather. The two bowls that had held water and brine shrimp were still right where she had put them, and the small dent where the bird had sat was clearly visible. Standing beside the box, Xandra surveyed the whole area carefully and decided that it hadn't changed and wasn't about to. Even though she waited for quite a long time, nothing at all happened, except that the anxious and fearful feeling she'd come in with gradually changed to disappointment. Yes, definitely disappointment that there wasn't at least a hint of friendly creatures of the Unseen. No creatures, and not even the slightest hint of threatening monsters.

Another long minute passed before Xandra suddenly reached for the string that held the feather. As she pulled it out from under her shirt, she was whispering to an imaginary Belinda, "Don't worry. I'm not going to do the forehead thing. I'm just going to hold it here in my hand while I put the other one right here where the bird sat. See? Just like you did when you were here."

She was still demonstrating and imagining Belinda's response when she suddenly became aware of something strange. A rustle first, a soft, brushing noise, and then a feathery puff of air against her cheek. Her hand, the one holding the feather, went to her cheek as she turned to follow the diminishing sound. Turned toward where, on top of the cabinet, a strange mix of shadow and splintered light was beginning to take on a familiar shape. The big-headed, flat-faced, round-eyed shape of a fledgling barn owl.

"Hey, Ratchet," she was whispering as she moved forward—but then it was gone. Nothing remained above the cabinet but a ray of dusty light. Several seconds went by as Xandra moved back to stand beside the white bird's nest and go on waiting and watching, but nothing more happened. At least nothing she could be sure of. There was an exciting moment or two when she thought she heard what sounded like the tiny, pitifully helpless cry of a very young kitten, and a little later she was able to get the slightest whiff of a smell that was vaguely reminiscent of Stinky's distinctive aroma.

The sights and sounds and smells were all uncertain but at that moment there was, for Xandra, one feeling that was becoming more and more certain. And the feeling was that something—or perhaps many somethings—was all around her. Many friendly creatures were very close by, even though she wasn't quite able to see and hear and touch them. Not able, at least, to see them the way she might if only . . .

Suddenly she pulled the string that held the feather up over her head, and grasping it in both hands, she held it high. And for a long moment she considered doing more. She felt sure she could do it. She could remember exactly the way Belinda had shown her to move her hands and then . . .

And then she stopped, as other memories began to

arise—distinct, vivid memories of all the terrible shapes and sounds, and the piercing, stabbing pain. And although she tried not to, she found herself recalling how the grandfather had said that no one had the use of a Key for very long, and that it was possible to be lost in the Unseen.

Shuddering, she hung the feather back around her neck and made her way past the furnace and then very quickly through the storage area and out into the morning daylight. Stopping briefly just outside the door, she turned to look back into the huge cluttered area that was the basement of the Hobson Habitat, and made a new promise. A promise this time to the friendly creatures of the Unseen that she was not leaving for good and always. That she would find a way to come back and see them again.

She would come back, she promised. However, there was, of course, only one way she could ever go back into her basement hideout and use the Key again—and that was for Belinda to come with her. Belinda had by now undoubtedly learned a great deal more from her wizard grandfather about all the things that might happen. Had even learned, perhaps, how the evil monsters could be held back and controlled.

That would be particularly interesting: if the evil creatures of the Unseen with their huge gaping mouths and glittering teeth could be clearly seen as they slunk around the edges of the storage room, but at the same time kept at a safe distance.

So the next step would be getting Belinda to talk to her again and make plans about what could be done and when it could happen. And when Monday morning finally arrived, Xandra was prepared to do exactly that.

She knew it wasn't going to be easy. Not easy, even though she no longer cared about not being seen talking to Belinda. As far as Xandra was concerned a meeting anywhere and anytime was fine. Early in the morning, perhaps, while everyone was arriving at school, or in the cafeteria at lunchtime or else in the classroom before Mr. Fernandez's arrival. Xandra was willing to approach Belinda in any of those places, and so she did. But the hard part turned out to be getting Belinda to answer important questions, or in fact to say anything at all except what she whispered over and over: "You mustn't use it anymore. Not ever anymore."

Standing beside Belinda's desk before the last bell rang, Xandra finally demanded angrily, "But why not? You said it would be all right after you found out more about how it works." But Belinda only bent her head over her language arts book and pretended to be reading. Xandra wanted to grab a handful of her long straggly hair and pull it hard, or else to push her book off the desk—wanted to, but didn't do it. But she was still in a yanking, pushing mood as she made her way back to her own desk On the way Marcie, *the* Marcie of Marcie's Mob herself, grabbed Xandra's arm and whispered, "What did she say? Did she say anything about me?" But Xandra only jerked her arm away and stomped on down the aisle.

That same day, late in the afternoon, Xandra paid an unplanned visit to the basement. It happened in a startling and entirely unexpected way. Xandra was just arriving home from school, walking down the driveway, when she heard something—a clattering, thumping noise that seemed to be coming from just around the corner, where the driveway curved into the garage. As she stopped to listen, there was a louder thump and then a high-pitched wail. A familiar high-pitched wail. When Xandra rounded the corner at a run, there she was: the little family favorite, lying on her stomach across a beat-up old skateboard, yelling her head off. Even after Xandra lifted her off the skateboard and sat her down, she went on yelling for a minute before she suddenly wiped her long-lashed doll-baby eyes with the palms of both hands, sniffed, smiled and said, "Hi, Xandra."

"Hi," Xandra said without smiling back. "Are you hurt?"

Still sniffing, Gussie examined her left knee and then her right elbow, both of which looked a little banged up but not much more than normal. "I guess not," she said. "I thought I was."

"Yeah, it sounded like it," Xandra said. She was about to ask, "When did you take up skateboarding?" when something familiar about the beat-up old skateboard made her change it to "Where did you get that thing?"

Gussie's tear-shiny face lit up like neon. "In the basement," she said. "I found a lot of good stuff down there. Like skateboards and scooters and all kinds of things like that."

Xandra stared in amazed alarm. "When?" she finally managed to ask. "When did you go in the basement? I mean, do you go in there a lot?"

Gussie thought for a moment before she said, "Oh yes. A lot. But not until today. Before today I peeked in some but it was too spooky. But today I went right on down the steps and I found all sorts of things to play with." Gussie's smile showed the space where one of her baby teeth had fallen out. "Did you know about all those things in the basement? Like this skateboard, and there's a scooter that's just a little bit broken and—"

"Yes, I know about it," Xandra interrupted. "It's just a lot of junk that nobody wants anymore."

"That nobody wants anymore?" It was Gussie's turn to sound amazed. After she'd thought for a minute, she went on, "Then why don't they give it to someone who does?"

Xandra tried a sarcastic smile, which of course Gussie didn't get. "Good question," she said. "I guess they think they might want it again someday." A sudden thought occurred to her. "Hey, where's Clara? Does Clara know where you are and what you're doing?"

Gussie's smile was a little bit sheepish. "Clara's taking a nap," she said.

"A nap?" Xandra looked at her watch.

Gussie was smiling again. "Not an on-purpose nap. Just a rocking chair one."

"Oh, I get it," Xandra said. "So Clara went to sleep and you skipped out. Well, I think you'd better get back in there before she wakes up and starts having a fit. Come on."

"No." Gussie tried to pull the skateboard out of Xandra's hands. "First I have to put this back where I got it."

But when Xandra said, "No, I'll do it," Gussie began to wail and say she had to do it herself. "I have to," she gulped. "I promised I would."

"You promised? Who'd you promise? What are you talking about?"

"I promised all the others. I promised all the rest of those things in there."

Shaken speechless by a sudden suspicion, Xandra stared and gasped before she grabbed Gussie by one of her skinny little arms and gave her a shake. "What kind of things did you see in the basement? What did they look like? Did they bite you?"

Gussie stared wide-eyed for a moment before she jumped up and ran.

15

XANDRA WAS HALFWAY up the stairs to the back door when she slowed down, stopped and gave up. Gave up trying to catch Gussie before somebody like Clara, or Geraldine, or one of the siblings appeared and wanted to know what was going on. Collapsing on the back steps, Xandra sat there imagining what the conversation might be like. Imagining what the rest of them might say if Gussie started blubbering about monsters with big teeth who lived in the basement. At last Xandra shrugged, sighed, went back to pick up the skateboard and headed for the basement door.

She was almost there, in fact reaching out for the latch, before she stopped to ask herself why. Why was she going into the basement? Well, she answered her own question, to take the skateboard back where it belonged so that . . .

A good reason would be . . . Yes, so that Gussie wouldn't get in trouble from whichever sibling it belonged to when they found it lying in the driveway. That was a perfectly respectable reason. But the other reason, the one that she was just on the edge of owning up to, was to find out who, or what, it was that Gussie had been talking to when she'd promised to bring the skateboard back.

She'd gotten about that far in her thinking and had started cautiously down the dimly lit flight of stairs, glancing nervously from side to side with every step when, without any warning at all, something grabbed her by the back of her shirt. Only halfway stifling a scream and dropping the skateboard, which clattered noisily on down the steps, Xandra whirled around to find herself face to face with . . . Gussie. Gussie was screaming too. Staring at Xandra with wide, unblinking eyes, Gussie shrieked loud enough to wake the dead. And went on screaming while Xandra's fright turned to quick relief and, then to exasperation. "Shut up, you little creep," she commanded. "Why are you yelling?"

Gussie's terror-stricken expression quickly changed to a wobbly smile. "Because you were. Why'd you do that?"

"Never mind that," Xandra said. "What are you doing back here? I thought you were looking for Clara."

Gussie nodded. "I was. But I didn't see her, so I decided to come and show you where it goes."

"Where what goes?" Xandra demanded.

"The skateboard." Gussie went down the steps, picked up the board and made her way down one of the narrow pathways to where a bunch of skis, scooters and other skateboards leaned against a far wall. "See?" she called back over her shoulder. "Here's where it lives. Right next to all its friends."

Xandra was beginning to have a sneaking suspicion that Gussie's promise to bring the skateboard back hadn't been made to a mysterious creature after all. At least not to the kind Xandra had in mind.

"Okay," she said. "When you said you promised to bring it back, what did you mean? Who did you promise?"

On her way back to the stairs Gussie stopped long enough to consider Xandra's question before she nodded. "I promised its friends I'd bring it right back so they wouldn't feel bad because they didn't get to go too."

"Friends?" Xandra asked.

"Its friends." Gussie pointed. "The other skateboards and the scooter and . . ."

Throwing up her hands in disgust, Xandra said, "Okay, okay, I get it." She did get it and she was about to use a bunch of words like "stupid" and "ridiculous" until something made her remember that Gussie wasn't the only one who sometimes talked to inanimate objects. Objects like stuffed toy animals, for instance, who, you had to admit, weren't much better conversationalists than skateboards and scooters.

At the top of the steps Gussie turned to take a last long look behind her. "There sure is a lot of stuff in here."

Xandra pulled her out of the way and shut and latched the door. "Yeah, I know," she said. "A lot of stuff. And you think we ought to . . ." She was about to repeat what Gussie had said about giving it away when a sudden idea interrupted her train of thought—an idea that just might be a useful topic of conversation the next time she tried to get Belinda to talk to her.

Xandra was tucking that idea away for future use when Gussie asked another question. One that needed a more immediate answer. They were inside the house by then, halfway down the back hall, when Gussie stopped and asked, "Is there something in the basement that bites? Why did you ask if something bit me?"

The first idea that flitted through Xandra's mind was *rats.* She could tell Gussie that there were big rats in the basement and that rats sometimes bit people. That might even scare her enough to keep her out of what had always been Xandra's very private territory. But something, perhaps Gussie's wide-eyed stare, made Xandra decide against the rat story. Instead what she said was the truth, or at least part of it. "I don't know for sure. It's just that once when I was in the basement, I had this feeling something was biting me. I wasn't sure what it was because I didn't quite see it, but I really thought something was biting me."

"Oh." Gussie nodded. "Like a mosquito, maybe?"

Gritting her teeth to keep from yelling, "No. Not anything like a mosquito," Xandra took a deep breath before she grated out, "Yeah, something like that, I guess."

Anyway it worked. At least Gussie stopped asking questions and when Clara came down the hall looking worried and half-asleep, nobody mentioned the basement or skateboards or even vacuum cleaners. But vacuum cleaners were still very much on Xandra's mind the next morning when Belinda got off the bus in front of the school.

"Hey," Xandra said when she caught up with Belinda as she was heading for the front entrance. "I have something important to tell you. Something you might like to know about."

Belinda didn't stop walking but she did turn her head. "What might I like to know about?"

"Well, it's just that . . ." Xandra was thinking and talking fast. "You remember all those vacuum cleaners that you saw in our basement, and I told you we don't use them anymore because my mother hired a cleaning service? Well, we're going to get rid of them pretty soon and I was wondering if . . ."

"Why are you going to get rid of them?" Belinda asked.

"Well, because the basement is just getting too crowded. There's no more room. And I remembered that you said you used to have one at the commune but it broke, and I was just wondering if you'd like to have one again."

Belinda stopped walking and turned to face Xandra. She looked suspicious but at the same time interested. In fact there was something about the way her dark eyes suddenly focused that made it perfectly clear that having a vacuum cleaner again was something she'd definitely thought about. "Yes," she said after a moment. "I would like to have a vacuum cleaner again, but how would it happen? I mean, how would I get it way out there? To the commune?"

Xandra hadn't thought about that. So far, finding a way to convince Belinda that she should come back to the Hobson basement was about as far as her plans had gone. But now, thinking fast, she came up with "Well, some of the newest ones aren't awfully heavy. The two of us together could carry it as far as the bus stop and then . . ."

"I don't know." Belinda's raised eyebrows and doubtful smile made the point that getting the vacuum cleaner to the bus stop didn't entirely solve the problem. "People might think I stole it." But Xandra wasn't finished. "I know," she said. "I could get a lot of that heavy brown wrapping paper and some tape and we could wrap it all up so people would think it was something you just bought at a store. And then . . ." She bogged down again but only for a minute. "And then you could use one of those little two-wheeled shopping carts. I've seen people bring those on buses and I'm pretty sure there's one of those someplace in the basement. And we could wrap the vacuum cleaner up and—"

Belinda interrupted her to say excitedly, "Ezra has one of those carts. He uses it when he goes shopping to bring the groceries up the hill to the house." And the way Belinda looked and sounded told Xandra that her plan was going to work. Belinda was going to agree to come back to Xandra's house, and the two of them together were, once again, going to go into the basement.

And then what? Xandra's thinking hadn't gotten that far and she wasn't going to let it. She had the feeling that if she let herself work out exactly what she might do next, Belinda or maybe the grandfather might be able, in some mysterious way like ESP or mind reading, to learn exactly what she was planning and do something to prevent it.

So that was how it happened. The very next afternoon Xandra, still dressed in her school clothes, went down the steps into the dimly lit basement. She was carrying a bunch of tape and wrapping paper and right behind her was Belinda, pushing Ezra's little two-wheeled shopping cart. So Xandra's clever and only slightly sneaky plan had worked. Belinda was back in the basement.

16

"OKAY, WHICH ONE do you want?" Xandra asked as the shopping cart bounced down the last basement step.

There was something about the way Belinda answered, "Which one? You mean I can have whichever one I like best?" that made Xandra think of the way a little kid like Gussie would sound if you took her into a toy store and said, "Take your pick." So that was exactly what she said to Belinda.

"Sure." Her sweeping motion took in the whole area. "Take your pick." And that was all she needed to say for a long time. As Belinda lined up vacuum cleaners and went from one to another, checking out each one carefully and thoroughly, Xandra stood back where she could keep an eye not only on Belinda, but also on whatever else might be going on in the farthest dark corners and the shadowy passageways between stacks of boxes.

So while Belinda wound and unwound electric cords and fiddled with all sorts of attachments, Xandra kept an eye out for . . . creatures of the Unseen, or whatever you wanted to call them. But nothing had happened by the time Belinda made her final selection, at least not for sure. There had been a couple of times when Xandra had been able, by squinting her eyes almost shut, to see, or almost see, something that looked like a moving shadow or a momentary slash of fiery light. But nothing for sure. She was still squinting, watching what seemed to be a shadowy figure against the right-hand wall, when Belinda tapped her on the left shoulder and said, "Okay. I think I've decided."

"Oh!" Xandra jumped and swallowed hard before she could say, "Oh. That one? Okay. Let's wrap it up."

While they taped wrapping paper around the chosen vacuum, Belinda did quite a lot of talking. At least quite a lot compared to the amount she'd been doing recently. Mostly she talked about how much easier it was going to be to keep both of the cabins clean now that she had a vacuum cleaner.

"And Ezra's house too," she said, smiling ruefully. "You wouldn't believe how dirty that big old house is."

"Do you have to clean his house too?" Xandra was shocked.

Belinda shook her head. "I don't have to, but I tried to once. That was when our old vacuum cleaner broke. I think it was Ezra's house that finished it off."

That stopped Xandra for a moment while she considered what it would be like to have to clean two cabins and a big superdirty house. It wasn't an easy thing to imagine for someone who had never cleaned her own room, except for now and then having to pile all her animals back on the bed when an extra-fussy cleaning lady insisted. Thinking about what a big help the vacuum was going to be, she really was feeling good about what she was doing, congratulating herself on doing such a good deed, without bothering to remember that it had been Gussie who gave her the idea. And for about the same length of time she also forgot the real reason they were in the basement.

Suddenly remembering, just as they had finished stuffing the carefully wrapped vacuum into the shopping cart, she said, "Okay, it's all ready. But now there's something I want you to do for me."

"All right. What do you want me to do?" Belinda's smile was wide and friendly, but when Xandra told her what she wanted, it quickly faded. "No," she said, frowning and shaking her head. "I can't. I won't."

Fighting down the familiar flush of anger, Xandra tried to be reasonable and convincing as she started to tell Belinda about the good, friendly creatures she had sensed when she had only held the Key in her hand, in her own room and again in the secret hideout behind the furnace. "I didn't really do it, because I promised you I wouldn't, but I held it like this"—she pulled the feather out from under her sweater—"and something, some good, friendly things were almost there and there weren't any of those—those other creatures."

But Belinda just went on shaking her head and refusing to listen or even to explain why she was being so stubborn.

When the rush of anger was too strong to resist,

Xandra almost yelled, "Why not? You told me it would be all right after you learned more about how to do it. Haven't you learned anything by now?"

Belinda's nod was slow in coming. Slow and uncertain. "Yes," she said reluctantly. "I learned why it would be so dangerous for *you* to do it again."

"So dangerous for *me*." Xandra copied the emphasis that made it clear that she was the only one Belinda was talking about. There she was, doing it again. Saying that using an enchanted gift would be all right for most people but not for Xandra. All right for everybody *except* Xandra, maybe. Like everything else that most people could do, or be, but not Xandra Hobson.

Grabbing the cart away from Belinda, Xandra dumped the vacuum cleaner out on the floor. Then she stomped up the stairs, out the basement door and around the house to the back door. She was still stomping when she got to the landing where a window looked down on the long curved driveway, from which it was possible to see who was arriving at the Hobsons' house—or leaving it. And sure enough, there she was. There went the creepy granddaughter of an even creepier old man, pushing her shopping cart as she turned out onto the avenue. An empty shopping cart. Xandra was gritting her teeth and telling herself, "It serves her right," as she turned quickly away and went up the stairs.

It was right then, while she was still fuming about Belinda, that Xandra began to hear loud noises. She'd only gone a few feet down the upstairs hall when she saw why. The door leading to the room of the Twinster sibling named Nelson was wide open, and noises weren't the only things coming through it. Along with shouts and loud laughter, also coming out through the open door, and stretching clear across the hall, was a long strip of bright green artificial grass. Just as Xandra approached the grass, a little white ball came rolling toward her. She knew what it was, of course. She recognized it immediately as the putting practice green that had been one of Quincy's favorite presents on his eighteenth birthday. And she also knew how special and private it was to Quincy, who had finally found a sport he might be as good at, or almost as good at, as his superjock brothers.

Afterward, a long time afterward, it occurred to Xandra that she might have just ignored the fact that the Twinsters were, as usual, up to no good. She might have stepped over the strip of putting green and gone on down the hall—if she hadn't been angry already. But she was angry—at Belinda and her grandfather, and more or less at the whole world.

And so, as loud teenage voices yelled, "Good shot," and, "Way to go, Nicko," Xandra stuck one foot in front of the golf ball, picked it up and walked down the strip of grass to the door. And there they were, a whole roomful of teenage boys: the two Twinsters and three of their friends. One of the Twinsters, Nicholas, apparently, was standing over the grass strip holding a putter, and four other long-legged teenagers were draped across the floor and over various pieces of furniture. There was a split second of quiet when Xandra appeared in the doorway and then a chorus of remarks like "Uh-oh, a kid-sister hazard," "Too bad, you lose" and "There goes your trophy, Hobson."

Nicholas grabbed Xandra's hand, took away the golf

ball and pulled her into the room. "Tell them," he yelled. "It *was* about to go into the cup, wasn't it, Alexandra? You saw it. You tell them."

Xandra shrugged. "I don't know where it was going," she said. She stared up at Nicholas and then turned to look at Nelson. "I thought Quincy said nobody could use his putting game," she said coldly. "I'm going to tell him." She'd turned around to walk out of the room and would have, except that Nicholas hadn't turned loose of her arm.

And then Nelson grabbed her other arm and dragged her back into the room and everyone began yelling at her. Yelling things like "Wow, what's eating you, kid?" and "Nothing like having a live-in stool pigeon." And "Why don't you tape her mouth shut, Hobson?"

Then Nicholas was saying, "Okay. Good idea. Here. Hold her a minute."

One of the others, a tall skinny guy with lots of acne, grabbed her left arm and he and Nelson held her while Nicholas went away and came back with a roll of the kind of heavy tape that gets wrapped around the handles of baseball bats. Nicholas was heading in her direction and pulling loose a long strip of tape when Xandra managed to kick one guy hard enough to make him turn loose of her arm and grab his wounded ankle. Then she socked Nelson on the chin, pulled her right arm free and ran for the door. But Nicholas yelled at the other guys to catch her and they did. Catching her by her arms and hair, they dragged her across the room while she fought back, kicking and slugging as hard as she could. Then somebody stuck out a foot and tripped her and she was on the floor and they were all holding her down while Nicholas started to stretch the nasty-tasting tape across her mouth.

She wasn't afraid. Not for a minute. It wasn't that she didn't think they might really hurt her. In fact she was far too angry to think anything at all. Her mind was full of nothing but boiling, swelling rage, and she was still fighting, kicking, squirming and trying to bite—when suddenly everything went quiet. Jerking her arms free, Xandra sat up, turned around and saw Clara standing in the doorway.

Clara was just standing there, not saying anything at all, while Nelson said, "Hi, Clara. We were just playing with her. We weren't going to hurt her." Nicholas started saying something about how she had kicked his golf ball just as he was about to win the game. Xandra didn't say anything, but as she started for the door, she stopped long enough to give the last guy to turn her loose a hard kick in the shin. Then she pushed past Clara and ran down the hall.

17

INSIDE HER OWN room Xandra slammed the door shut and leaned against it, breathing hard and waiting. Waiting for Clara to knock so she could open the door only a crack and say, "I'm okay. I just want to be by myself for a while." The knock came, just as Xandra was sure it would, and she said what she'd planned to say. Then she had to say it again more loudly and add, "Go away. I don't want to talk about it."

She waited until Clara had finished saying a bunch of other stuff about where she would be when Xandra felt like talking, and how she'd talked to the boys but she wanted to hear Xandra's side of it before she talked to their parents. After Clara finally went away, Xandra opened the door a crack to watch her leave. It wasn't until Clara was out of sight that Xandra ran to her bed and climbed in among her animals.

But that didn't help either. Not this time. Even when her head was pillowed on soft, velvety animals of all shapes and sizes, and dozens of others were clutched against her chest. This time, which animals happened to be on top of the pile, and how she felt about them, didn't make any difference. In fact the only thing that mattered was how rotten and mean and treacherous the Twinsters were, and how their friends were even worse, and how much she hated all of them. And worst of all was Belinda, because she was a liar, and the things she said about the enchanted feather and the Unseen creatures were just lies she thought up to make Xandra feel as if everything bad that had happened was all her fault, and as if it would be safe for anyone else to have a Key, but not for Xandra Hobson.

Suddenly Xandra sat straight up, scattering animals in every direction. As a displaced skunk, an alligator, a dolphin, a moose, a tiger and any number of bears tumbled off the bed, she jumped up, ran down the hall and out of the house.

The sun was still fairly high in the western sky when Xandra ran down the back steps and around to the basement door. Around to the sleek, well-painted exterior of a door that, if opened, would reveal a huge clutter of dusty junk, around and behind which a dimly lit passageway led back to a shadowy corner. For a long time, maybe a minute or two, Xandra stood still staring at the door, but not because she was thinking and planning what she was going to do next. She was in no mood to think and plan. She was only waiting for something to push her. The same kind of push that had made her fight the twins and their friends so fiercely and had made her yell at Clara and tell her to go away. But when the push came in a sudden surge of rage, it wasn't toward the basement door, but out away from the house. Away from the house, through the back gate and out into the forest. She ran into the forest still wearing her school clothes and without any idea where she was heading or what she intended to do when she got there.

She went on running at first across the partly cleared land and then on into the forest on one of the pathways she had followed many times before. A path that twisted and turned around the edge of the marsh, and on between trees and underbrush to where it dropped down over the bank of Cascade Creek. The creek was wider and deeper now than it had been on the day Xandra had waded up it carrying the wounded bird, but she was able to cross it at the narrow spot where three large boulders served as stepping-stones. It wasn't until she'd run deep into the forest that her pace slowed and she finally came to a stop.

It was only then that she allowed herself to wonder what she was doing and why she was there. But wondering didn't bring answers—at least not ones that were clearly understandable. When Xandra began to ask herself where she was going, all she got was a series of vague thoughts and feelings. Old familiar thoughts that brought up expected responses.

She was in the forest because she had always loved being there—and nobody had the right to tell her not to go there. Certainly not Clara, who was only a baby-sitter, and not even Xandra's baby-sitter, at that. And not Henry or Helen, who probably had forgotten, if they'd ever known, that Xandra loved the forest. So she was there because no one had the right to tell her not to be. All right, that was part of the answer, even if it wasn't the most important part.

And what was she going to do now? That was harder, but it had something to do with the enchanted bird. Turning slowly in a circle, Xandra tried to decide if the small clearing she had just entered was the same one where she'd found the bird. Looking around at the small open space surrounded by overhanging trees, darkened now by lengthening shadows, she wasn't entirely sure it was the same place. She did remember that the clearing where she had found the bird had seemed larger and also deeper in the forest. But wasn't it possible that this was the one, the same small treeless meadow? And then there was the question of why she wanted to find the clearing, maybe even the exact spot, where the bird had been when she'd found and rescued it.

The answer to that one was even less clear and certain but it had something to do with another question that she needed to find an answer to. A question about why she'd been allowed to find and save the bird, and why she had been given the feather that Belinda called a Key. It had to have been for some particular reason. And it didn't make sense for the reason to be that she was somehow too different—too weak and stupid, maybe even too evil—to use it safely.

She suddenly remembered, remembered vividly, Belinda's exact words when she'd said, "It would be too dangerous for *you* to do it again." And with that memory came the certainty that what she was hearing was that everyone else was better and more special than she. And with that certainty came the quick, flaring anger that had made her take back the vacuum cleaner and charge into the house, where the twins and their friends had treated her as if she were . . . As if she were what? Some kind of less-than-human nuisance to be teased and tormented in insulting and embarrassing ways.

At that point, without stopping to think, without even asking herself what she meant to do, Xandra reached under her sweater and pulled out the enchanted feather. When she had it in both her hands, she closed her eyes, lifted it over her head and pressed it briefly to her forehead, before quickly hanging it back around her neck.

It was then, while the strange sensation of growing and stretching was just beginning, that she was suddenly terribly frightened. So frightened that for a moment she wished desperately that she could stop what was happening. She was about to retrieve the feather and try to undo what she had done when the fear began to turn into a strange eager excitement.

This time sounds came first. Even before she opened her eyes, she became aware that she was hearing all sorts of noises. Familiar sounds, like birdcalls and the stirring of branches in a soft breeze, only suddenly louder and far clearer and more distinct. And then other noises, more distant but strangely threatening, like faraway muttering cries and angry buzzes. And smells too. Sharp, caustic odors like smoke drifting from the embers of fires that had burned strange, unnatural fuels.

Opening her eyes was difficult at first, almost painful, but what she saw as they opened wider was fascinating—and then terrifying. All around her the forest itself was weirdly beautiful in a sparkling, sharp-edged way, as if every leaf and twig were clearly and distinctly visible. Visible and at the same time almost transparent, so that if you looked closely, you could see into and through everything you focused on—see the veins pulsing through each leaf, tiny, microscopic insects crawling everywhere and sap oozing up and down inside the trunks of the trees.

Xandra turned in a slow circle, focusing upward at first on leaves that glittered with growing, flowing life, and then down to the forest floor, where tiny creatures she'd never seen before were scurrying in all directions. She was kneeling, staring in wonder at the ground around her, when the strange muttering sounds, louder now and closer, brought her quickly to her feet.

It was then that she began to see what had been Unseen. Shapes and shadows moving through the undergrowth and between the trunks of trees, close by and coming closer. Nothing more than clumps of darkness at first, but with swiftly changing outlines, which as they came nearer began to condense into definite forms and figures. Some of the creatures of the Unseen were animal-like, sinister humpbacked shadows, like misshapen hyenas or bears. But others looked vaguely human. Short and stooped, but definitely upright figures, draped in hooded robes. And all of them seemed to be gliding smoothly through the underbrush that surrounded the clearing.

Gasping with fear, Xandra backed away as she desperately tried to pull the Key up from under her sweater where she could . . . Or could she? Even as she pressed the feather against her forehead, the humpbacked creatures moved closer as if . . . As if it was no longer working, just as Belinda had said it might happen.

Suddenly feeling terribly threatened, Xandra backed away and went on backing—out of the open clearing and down a narrow pathway between tall trees. Once out of sight of the monstrous figures, she turned and began to run. To run as fast as she could but, it soon became obvious, not fast enough. The creatures were running with her. She could hear their thudding footsteps, muttering, moaning voices and the snapping of twigs and swishing of branches as they ran beside her. Now and then she caught glimpses of humped backs and round-hooded heads. But she went on running until she tripped on a fallen tree limb and fell hard. Bruised and breathless, she scrambled to her feet and saw that it was too late. They were all around her.

On every side creatures of the Unseen oozed forward: humped and hooded almost-human shapes, and others that slithered across the ground like gigantic worms. Supported by their strange bloated bodies, their huge heads were almost faceless except for flaming eyes and the sharp, metallic glitter of teeth. And then they were attacking, just as they had done before.

Just as before, Xandra first smelled the awful stench of their breath, and almost immediately afterward, she began to feel their razor-sharp teeth. The teeth slashed and stabbed, ripping into her arms and legs and then her face and neck. She fought back, screaming in pain and hitting out with both fists. Striking out as hard as she could, she felt her knuckles thudding into objects that gave way under the blows and then once more surged forward. But although she struck again and again, and now and then the creatures seemed to fall back as if she had succeeded in fighting them off, a moment later they were back as fiercely punishing as ever. And once again she felt the fiery pain of their attacks. At last, when it became horribly clear that she would not be able to drive them away, she began to scream.

"Help," she shrieked. "Help me."

Her screams seemed to go on and on, repeating themselves as they echoed through the air, splintering into thin metallic sounds shredded by the jewel-sharp edges of the surrounding leaves and branches. "Help," Xandra cried, and her cries spread and multiplied as they reverberated through the forest. Over and over again, "Help. Help me."

Xandra was still screaming when something soft and swift brushed against her face, and turning her head to follow its touch, she saw a feathery wisp of light drifting away from her down a narrow passageway. Forcing her way between clinging, slashing clumps of darkness, she ran, following the feathered phantom. Once again she was running, following fleeting glimpses of winglike shafts of light, down a path that turned, twisted and broke out into a small meadow. A clearing that this time she recognized immediately and with absolute certainty. It was the place where she had found the white bird.

This time there was no doubt. The flat, almost circular open space was surrounded by tall trees, and there, just before her, was the fern-covered mound where the wounded bird had fallen. Staggering forward, Xandra collapsed, reaching out with both hands toward the mound.

Sometime afterward, how long she couldn't even guess, she became aware that all around her there were sounds and movements, but the sounds were not growls or moans, and the movements she was sensing didn't seem to be rapid or violent. But still, something was there.

Pushing herself to a sitting position, she glanced fearfully from side to side, but there was nothing to see except a carpet of ferns and vines encircled by tall trees. Vines and trees whose leaves glittered and pulsed with life, which meant that she was still in the world of the Unseen. But an Unseen that here in the white bird's meadow was not the same. The difference was everywhere, in the gentle touch of the breeze and the soft musky odors it carried. As well as in the absence of dark-robed creatures creeping toward her over the forest floor. No shadowy dark-robed shapes anywhere at all, and yet she felt she was not alone.

18

SITTING AMONG THE vines in the white bird's meadow, and hugging her knees against her chest, Xandra stared long and carefully in every direction. That she was still in the world of the Unseen was obvious. All around her the forest sparkled and surged with life, as did every strand of ivy and fern that covered the forest floor. And although the savage creatures were no longer attacking, the pain from their bites still throbbed and burned all over her body. Yes, the injuries were still unhealed. All over her arms and legs, and on her face and neck too, the wounds were raw and painful. But where were her attackers now? Where had they gone and why had they stopped tormenting her?

It was then that she began to guess why she was no longer being attacked. Just as the evil monsters had not entered her secret animal shelter behind the furnace, the white bird's meadow might also be a refuge, a peaceful sanctuary. And yet, why did she feel so certain that something probably as strange, and perhaps as dangerous, was close by and coming closer?

But this time the first creatures she actually saw—saw well enough to be certain—were very small. Creatures of the Unseen to be sure, vaguely defined and of uncertain shape, but with faces that were more than flaming eyes and slashing teeth. These small creatures were round-eyed and furry-faced, with damp twitchy noses and ears that flopped or flared. And there was at least one that flew, that soared across the clearing and back again and, at last, settled down on a low limb of the nearest tree. Turning his round, flat face from side to side, he opened his hooked beak and emitted his noisy clattering call.

"Ratchet." Xandra jumped to her feet and started in his direction, only to see him flutter and fade from view. "Come back, Ratchet," she called after him. "I knew it was you. I knew it all the time." And she had known, or at least had almost guessed, that it had been Ratchet that led her away from the evil Unseen and into the safety of the white bird's clearing.

But Ratchet had disappeared. However, as Xandra turned back into the center of the open area, she became aware of another very small creature. In fact, several of them. As she walked slowly back to the mound, they seemed to be frolicking around her like a bunch of romping kittens. Yes, exactly like the very young kittens she'd found in a ditch beside Heritage Avenue and had raised to an age when they could be adopted out to friends and friends of friends. Remembering how cute they'd been and how much she'd hated to part with them, she sat down quickly, whispering the names she had given them.

"Muffet," she whispered toward one prim pink-nosed face. "And there you are, Puzzle. I see you too."

They seemed to hear. Each of them whose name she called paused, stared at Xandra and then skittered off and a moment later was replaced by another creature. The next one she recognized was Stinky for sure, his distinctive white stripe as noticeable as ever, running the length of his little black body and extending out to the end of his tail. And the aroma was Stinky too. More delicate perhaps now, but just as delightfully disgusting as ever. And the slow, self-confident, don't-fool-with-me gait was definitely his too. When Xandra held out her hand, he came closer, closer than any of the other friendly Unseen had until that moment.

When Stinky's shiny black nose touched her fingers, she turned her hand over and let him sniff the palm, just as he had always done, looking for a marshmallow or a handful of kibble. But now he came even closer, moving his searching nose up her arm until it stopped over one of the ugly wounds left by the bites of the monsters. Stopped, sniffed and then raised his tail indignantly as he had always done when something displeased him.

"I know," Xandra said. "They bit me. Those ugly things bit me. But you wouldn't, would you?"

When she reached out to touch him, he faded away, but then he was back again and this time he allowed her to touch his warm silky head. She was still enjoying the warm reality of his presence when she noticed the approach of another familiar shape. The softly slithering shape of a friendly garter snake. And along with Stinky and the snake there soon appeared another batch of romping kittens, as well as a flock of birds, sparrows and mockingbirds and one large and noisy blue jay—all the different kinds of birds she had raised, or at least tried to raise, from fledglings. And then Ratchet appeared again, down to earth now and stalking with owlish dignity on his great clawed feet.

The friendly creatures were bolder now, allowing her to touch and caress them. Lying back on the soft bed of ivy and ferns, Xandra gathered up armfuls of animals, just as she did in bed every night, except that these animals, as warm and real as they seemed for the moment, were only phantoms of the Unseen called up from formlessness by . . . by what? What brought them? How long would they stay? And when they had gone—what then? Suddenly Xandra sat up, shaking off a cluster of warmly cuddling creatures.

Around the white bird's sanctuary were many acres of surrounding forest. A forest where the deep shade was now swiftly fading toward a moonless night. Even now, with the sharply penetrating vision produced by the Key, Xandra was unable to see beyond the surrounding circle of trees. Looking at her watch, she gasped. If she didn't move quickly, she would soon be deep in the forest in the dark of night.

After quickly removing the remaining kittens from her lap, Xandra got to her feet and started off in the direction of the path she had been following when she had entered the clearing. She started, paused, looked around and came back to where she had begun.

"Ratchet," she called. "Stinky. Come with me. Show me the way back to where I came from."

The owl answered her call almost immediately, but when he reappeared, he only swooped down to land in the center of the clearing, where he moved in a small circle with stubborn solemnity. He paid no attention when Xandra urged him to "fly toward home, Ratchet. Fly to where I used to feed you. Go on, fly." Even when she stomped her feet and waved her arms at him, he refused to take to the air.

And Stinky was even less helpful. Appearing suddenly at her side, he planted himself in one spot and stubbornly refused to budge. Finally, in desperation Xandra decided to go it alone, but when she started off toward the beginning of the path, it became obvious that Stinky and Ratchet were trying to force her to stay where she was. Stinky moved only enough to get in front of her, and with lowered head and raised tail he seemed to be threatening what he might do if she kept going. And when Ratchet finally took to the air, it was only to swoop around her head, close enough to make her throw up her arms to protect her face from his beating wings.

"Look," she told them, "I have to go home. Why won't you let me?"

There was, of course, no answer. Animals of the Unseen, it seemed, were no more talkative than were the stuffed variety. Except that now her ears had begun to hear, or at least to feel, something. To feel a message that came perhaps from Stinky and Ratchet and seemed to be saying it would be dangerous for her to leave. A message that she simply had to ignore.

"No," she called to the hovering owl. "It will be all right. See?" She gestured around the clearing. "They're gone. The monsters are all gone. And I do have to get home."

Jumping over Stinky and ducking Ratchet's beating wings, she started down the path at a run. But she had only gone a few yards when her impatience turned to fear.

Once again she was aware that something was running beside her. From both sides of the pathway, crackling branches and savage, growling grunts warned that the monsters of the Unseen had returned. She tried to run faster, but on the narrow, twisting pathways it was now almost completely dark. After thudding painfully into tree trunks and scratchy brambles, she came to a stop and was immediately surrounded by fiery eyes and the glitter of razor sharp teeth.

There was still the Key—but would it help? It had failed once before. But now, as the stabbing teeth attacked, she managed to raise her arms enough to reach under her sweater, retrieve the feather and pull it up to where she could enclose it in both hands.

It was later, perhaps only a few seconds, or possibly as much as several minutes, when Xandra became aware that she was lying on the forest floor. Lying on the cold forest floor, and all around her there was only silence and darkness.

19

PUSHING HERSELF SLOWLY and cautiously to a sitting position, Xandra turned her head from side to side and saw . . . nothing at all. For a terrifying moment she thought she had been struck blind until she glanced up to where the night sky still showed a faded hint of sunset. But down on the forest floor, where she was sitting on what felt like a carpet of pine needles, there was only darkness. Complete, absolute and absolutely terrifying darkness. However, as she slowly began to realize, there were at least no threatening snarls or moans and no flashing eyes and teeth. She had escaped the Unseen.

And the terrible sharp pains left by the evil creatures' teeth? Suddenly becoming aware that she was no longer in pain, Xandra ran her hands over her arms first and then her legs and found no trace of the deep wounds. All the painful punctures that had tormented her even in the relative safety of the white bird's clearing now seemed to have disappeared. Had suddenly, magically healed, just as they had on that other day, when Belinda had shown her how to enter the world of the Unseen and then how to escape from it. And now, just as before, the wounds had disappeared, leaving only a slight itchy tingle where they once had been, raw and damp with blood.

So Xandra Hobson was safely back in the real world and for a moment she felt so relieved that she almost laughed out loud. Just for a very brief moment, though, before it became only too obvious that she still had some very serious problems. Problems like having missed dinner, which meant she would have been called first, and then looked for, and then . . . Then what?

She could imagine only too clearly what questions would have been asked and answered, by Clara and of course by the Twinsters, and what they might have said about the kicked golf ball and the fight that followed. And how what they said might have influenced the parents' decision concerning what should be done about their missing daughter. What should be done, and how soon they would have to do it. Remembering how more than once in the past, when she'd been particularly angry at someone, she had hidden out and refused to come to dinner, it occurred to Xandra that it was possible that nothing at all had been done, at least not yet. Not while the whole family was still waiting for her to come to her senses and come out of the linen closet or perhaps the attic, or wherever it was that she happened to be hiding this time.

The other more urgent problem was that she was alone

somewhere in the middle of the forest on a dark night. On a very dark, very cold night. Not to mention, and not even to think about, if you could help it, a forest that might be full of dangerous real-life creatures. Mountain lions, perhaps, or rattlesnakes or some of the other dangerous things that, according to the twins, made their homes in the nearby hills and often came down to Xandra's forest to hunt for birds or rabbits, or other equally helpless victims.

Getting quickly to her feet, Xandra shuffled forward, reaching out blindly until her hands contacted a thicket of bushes. Scratchy, thorny blackberry bushes that pricked her fingers and obviously would tear her to pieces if she tried to push her way through. She turned back then and moved slowly in another direction, groping blindly until her hands found what seemed to be the trunk of a large tree. She was feeling her way around it when she suddenly visualized the trunk crawling with biting ants or poisonous spiders. Snatching her hands away, she moved on, only to stumble over something, an exposed root or a large rock, and fall to her knees.

But she kept on trying. Shivering now from the cold as well as from fear, she felt her way around tree trunks and bushes, trying to find an open pathway that might take her to . . . To where? Where did she think she was going? She had been shuffling in first one direction and then another, for a period of time that might have been a few very long minutes or even as much as an hour, when she began to accept that what she was doing was not only dangerous but entirely useless. Any sort of movement might very well be taking her farther away from home. There really was no point in trying to go anywhere until daylight returned.

She stopped then, or at least stopped moving in any particular direction. Instead she began to shuffle around in a small circle, stomping her feet, claiming a small spot the way dogs do before they lie down. Why? Who knows? Maybe it was something to do with the fact that she had always been so enchanted by animals, so used to thinking of herself as a half human, half animal. Or maybe she had just used her human mind to figure out that it would be a good idea to kill or scare away any ants or spiders that happened to be in the immediate vicinity before she sat down. Sat down to wait for daylight.

The waiting was long and terrible. Terribly lonely, terribly frightening and terribly uncomfortable. She sat upright at first with her knees pulled up against her chest, her skirt tucked around her legs and her arms wrapped around her knees. But a fairly heavy sweater, which was fine for daytime wear in late autumn, was not nearly warm enough under the circumstances. Clenching her teeth against their helpless chattering, she rested her head on her knees and tried counting slowly to one hundred and then backward again to zero. And then over again to one hundred, and back again. She didn't know why. It was something she usually did when she couldn't sleep at night, but now, when there was no hope of sleeping, it was only a way to try to convince herself that time was passing.

Now and then she held up her left arm and tried to see her watch but the darkness was so complete that she was unable to make out even the shape of the watch itself, let alone its hands and numbers. Time, she supposed, was actually passing but there was no way to tell how much of it had passed, or how long it would be until morning. Now and then she almost slept, or at least dozed a little and then woke with a start as she started to tip sideways or lose her grip on her knees. And as every slow minute passed, the cold became more and more unbearable.

In between and even worse than the spells of counting and dozing were the moments of wide-awake alertness. Moments in which she repeatedly turned her head from side to side, listening intently and hearing . . . almost nothing. Hearing nothing more than a faint rustling, only a breath of wind in the branches above her head—or the stealthy approach of a mountain lion? Or perhaps only sensing the presence of invisible, unformed shapes of the Unseen. Forms that were, according to Belinda, "always there, always everywhere." Constantly changing shapes that were around everyone, just waiting for a Key to bring them into fierce, painful reality.

The Key. Thinking about it, imagining it hanging there under her sweater, Xandra could feel, or at least imagine that she felt, a tiny area of warmth in the center of her chest. But she was not tempted to pull on the string that held it. The memory of what it had done, what it had caused to happen, was too fresh in her mind. As terrible as things were at the moment, as much as she was threatened by the cold, and the real-life dangers of the nighttime forest, it was not nearly as bad as the possibility of another attack by the evil creatures of the Unseen world. Instead she only pressed her freezing hands against her chest and imagined that, even through the sweater, she could feel a slight echo of the feather's warmth and power.

Later, probably much later, coming up out of a period of semiconsciousness, Xandra opened her eyes to a slight change in the density of the surrounding darkness. True, it was still very dark in her immediate vicinity, but looking up, she could now see that in one direction the sky had become a little more transparent. Sunrise was on the way and with it came some idea of east and west. Knowing that sunrise was in the east, and that the Hobson Habitat was directly to the east of the forest, Xandra knew in what direction she should try to move. Stumbling to her feet, she began to shuffle toward the light.

At first her progress was very slow. In areas where the forest canopy was heavy, she still had to feel her way, continuing to head in the right direction only by catching glimpses now and then of the brightening eastern sky. But as the long minutes of slow, shuffling progress crept by, the light increased, making it possible for her to find trails and then familiar pathways. By the time she reached the area where a familiar slope led down to Cascade Creek, she was almost running. It was then, while she was skidding down the slope toward the stream, that she stepped on a loose rock, tripped and fell hard, twisting her left ankle.

The pain was awful. So bad that for a time she was not aware of anything else. As she lay on her side, clutching her ankle, with her eyes squeezed shut, her mind was emptied of thought and memory. Perhaps she was crying, or even screaming, as they claimed afterward. She couldn't remember. But she would always remember what they said when they found her.

20

LYING ON THE RIVERBANK, clutching her ankle and crying, maybe screaming, the first thing she heard was Nicholas, or else it was Nelson, saying, "Hey. Look what I found. We thought you'd be out here somewhere."

And then the other one, Nelson or else Nicholas, said, "You can stop yelling now. You're about to be rescued."

And when she opened her eyes, there they were bending over her. And for once the two of them, two Greek-god faces under helmets of curly blond hair, did look amazingly beautiful. In fact, just about the most beautiful thing Xandra ever remembered seeing in her whole life. Still clutching her ankle, she caught her breath and managed to say, "Hi." And then, "It's my leg. I think it's broken."

"Oh yeah?" One of them, Nelson it turned out to be,

grabbed her shoulders and lifted her to a sitting position. "Look at her leg, Nick."

So it must have been Nicholas who knelt down and peeled her fingers off her wounded leg. "Here, let me see," he said as he ran his fingers around her ankle.

"What do you think?" Nelson asked. "Is it broken?"

"I'm not sure," Nicholas said. "It might be. Or else sprained. Anyway I think it's starting to swell. You ought to have an ice pack, but right now . . ."

"Well, we could at least do a bandage," Nelson said. "I think we ought to do a bandage. You know, a figure-eight bandage." Releasing her ankle, he stood up, scratching his head as he looked around, looked around some more and then suddenly started unzipping his heavy jacket. He took the jacket off first, and then his shirt. And then, standing there naked to the waist in the freezing air, Nelson started ripping a good cotton shirt into long strips.

"Hey, good thinking," Nicholas said, and a second later he was tearing up his shirt too. And then there the Twinsters were, half naked in the awful cold, down on their knees wrapping Xandra's ankle in what remained of their shirts. It must have been a pretty weird scene, and later Xandra was amazed just remembering it. But right then, when it was actually happening, her mind didn't have much room for anything but pain.

The wrapping hurt, especially at first, but as the bandage got wider and firmer, the pain in her ankle did seem to become a little more bearable. But not the cold. Now that the ankle was feeling a little better, she was once more aware of how hard she was shaking and chattering. And looking at the goose bumps on her half-naked brothers wasn't helping at all.

"How's that?" Nicholas asked when the last strip of shirt had been wrapped and tied. "Any better?"

She nodded, held back a sob, nodded again and said, "Better." And then, "You'll freeze. Put on your jackets."

One of them, she'd lost track again, laughed and said, "Hey. Good thinking." But before he could get both arms into his jacket, the other one said, "No way, Nelson. We'll need both of them for the stretcher. You remember, don't you? The jacket stretcher."

"Hey. Yeah, you're right," Nelson said as they both disappeared into the bushes while Xandra sat there shaking and wondering what in the world they thought they were doing. But in a few minutes they were back, stripping the branches off two long straight saplings, which they proceeded to run through the sleeves of the jackets, all the time arguing about how to do whatever it was they were trying to do.

Shivering more and more violently as she watched them pulling the poles out of the sleeves, yelling at each other, putting the poles back in again and then having trouble getting the zippers pulled up, Xandra felt . . . well, okay, impatient, all right, but at the same time not quite as impatient as you might expect, considering that she was nearly frozen solid and about to die of a broken leg. But by the time the stretcher was finally put together, and she was being carried on it while the twins waded through the creek in their good shoes, the whole scene began to seem too weirdly outrageous to take seriously. With half-frozen tears still running down her cheeks, she began to laugh.

"Wha-wha-what's she doing n-now?" Nelson asked, looking back at her over his bare shoulder.

Nicholas's teeth were chattering too. "You g-g-got me. Hysterics, I guess."

Nelson began to grin. "Yeah, hys-hys-hys-t-t-terics," he said, and his exaggerated stammer made Nicholas laugh even harder. They were all three laughing wildly as they went up the back stairs and into the house, but when they got as far as the kitchen, the Twinsters only stopped long enough to lift Xandra off the jacket stretcher onto the kitchen floor and shout a few things like "Hey, everybody. Here she is. We found her." And then, "Come and get her. We're going to be late for practice." Then, taking their jackets with them, they disappeared.

Clara was the first one to show up, with Gussie right behind her. Dropping to her knees, Clara pulled Xandra into her arms, whispering, "Thank God. Oh, thank God," and then, "Are you all right, baby?"

Handicapped by her chattering teeth as well as the huge lump that had suddenly taken over her throat, Xandra could only nod. "All r-r-right. I'm all r-r-right," she finally managed.

Clara touched Xandra's hands and face and whispered, "But you're so cold, darling. You're just about frozen." And then Clara was on her feet and running out of the room, which left only Gussie. Gussie, still dressed in her flannel nightgown and clutching Debbie, her enormous life-sized doll, against her chest, was staring at Xandra with wide tearful eyes and whispering, "We were crying. Clara was crying and so were we."

"We?" Xandra asked. "Who else was crying?"

"We were." Gussie held out her doll. "Debbie and me." She was demonstrating, sniffing and sobbing and wiping imaginary tears off Debbie's big plastic face, when Clara ran back into the room carrying an armload of pillows and blankets and hot-water bottles. And while Clara filled hot-water bottles and arranged pillows and blankets, Gussie walked around them in a circle, dragging Debbie by one shoeless plastic foot and asking endless questions. Questions like "Where you been, Xandra? Why were we crying? Why are you lying on the floor?"

A few minutes later, when other people began to show up, Xandra was still on the kitchen floor but wrapped up like a mummy. Warmer now, and not in quite as much pain, she was having a hard time keeping her eyes open. The parents came in next, Helen first and then Henry. Henry's hair was on end and he was still in his bathrobe, but Helen seemed to be dressed for the courtroom, as always, and looking and acting more like a famous lawyer than someone who had just found her lost kid. But when she saw Xandra lying on the kitchen floor bundled up like a mummy, she did get a little less dignified-looking, at least for a minute. She even got down on the floor beside Xandra before she started asking lawyerish questions. Questions like "Where have you been?" And "Why?"

"Why"! Even before she got around to "How's your leg? The boys said you'd hurt it."

Then the doorbell was ringing and Henry left with Gussie running after him, and a minute later Gussie came back talking about policemen. Getting down on her hands and knees, she put her mouth near Xandra's ear and whispered, "There are two policemen in the hall talking to Daddy."

"Police?" Xandra asked her mother. "Why are the police here?" For an anxious moment she wondered if you could be put in jail for running away and getting lost.

Her mother was smiling as she got to her feet. "We called them a few minutes ago," she said, "when we realized you really were missing and not just . . ." Her smile disappeared as she went on, "and not just hiding out again."

The kitchen door opened and Henry came in, along with two policemen. And then both of the policemen were asking questions and everyone was answering them, even the ones that no one could really answer except Xandra herself.

"Yes," Henry said, "there was a misunderstanding with her brothers, and she must have run out of the house. . . ."

"A misunderstanding?" one of the policemen asked.

"Well, let's be accurate, Henry," Helen said. "According to Clara, here, who was the only eyewitness, it was a bit of a brawl." She smiled, showing all of her beautiful white teeth. "You know, Officer, the kind of intrafamily altercation most kids indulge in from time to time."

For a while no one asked Xandra to describe the "altercation" or what had happened afterward, but when one of the policemen knelt down beside her and asked, "Where were you? Where did you go?" she managed to answer, "Into the forest. I was lost in the forest."

His next question was "Who was with you? Did someone take you or meet you there?"

"No one was with me. No one took me there. I went by myself and got lost. And I think I broke my leg."

"Broke your leg? Then how did you get home?" the policeman asked.

"They found me. The same two brothers who beat up on . . . ," Xandra had begun when Helen took over and explained how two of her sons had gone out looking for their sister and had found her and brought her home. And when the policemen asked to talk to the rescuers, it was Henry who explained why they weren't there. He was chuckling as he said, "There was an important early-morning practice at the high school, and you fellows have probably heard about Coach Macafee's attitude toward missing a practice. I'm afraid the need to rescue a little sister with a broken leg wouldn't have gotten them out of Macafee's doghouse."

So then Clara unwrapped enough blankets to expose Xandra's injured leg, and everyone had to get down on the kitchen floor and examine it and say whether they thought it was broken or sprained, and all Xandra could do was wish they'd all go away and let her sleep. Victoria had turned up by then, and Quincy too, and both of them had to ask the same old questions and hear everybody's version of the answers. Xandra's ankle was still hurting some and she was feeling more and more exhausted and sleepy. She was on the verge of yelling, "Go away, all of you. Go away and leave me alone." But nobody left until the tall policeman said he didn't think he was needed any longer and that the next thing that ought to be done was to "get that child to a doctor." And even though she resented being called a child, Xandra was pleased with the result, which was that a lot of Hobsons left the room.

21

IT WAS CLARA who drove Xandra to the doctor's office. Henry himself was going to take her, but when Clara offered to do it, he quickly accepted. "Could you?" he said to Clara. "There's an important meeting this morning and there's a huge amount of due diligence that will need to be done beforehand."

Xandra wasn't sure what due diligence was, but it was obviously a lot more urgent than a broken leg. Particularly if the broken leg was no more than what a certain person deserved for running away and getting her leg broken and taking all the Hobsons' minds off more important things. That wasn't exactly what Henry said but it was pretty obvious that was what he was thinking. And what he went on thinking and hinting about while he carried Xandra out to Clara's car.

But at least Henry didn't ask any more questions about exactly where Xandra had been all night and what had happened there—questions that Xandra wasn't anywhere near being able to deal with as yet. And which she felt certain Clara would insist on asking as soon as they were in the car. But, to her surprise, it didn't happen. Clara only asked if she was ready to talk about it, and when Xandra shook her head, she didn't say anything more.

According to Dr. Frank, the ankle wasn't broken. Dr. Frank, who, for years and years, had treated everyone in the Hobson family for things like stomach upsets and sore throats, said it was only a bad sprain. He also said all the usual things about the talented and beautiful Hobsons, and then looked at Xandra as if he were thinking, "So where'd they find you, kid?" After he'd rewrapped her ankle in a kind of removable cast, he brought out some crutches and had her try them out for size. "There you are, young lady," he said cheerfully. "Wrap that ankle in an ice pack for the rest of the day, and then with just a few more days at home with your foot up, maybe even by Thursday or Friday of next week, you should be able to go back to school. That is, if you use the crutches and promise not to try to walk on that bum foot for a couple of weeks."

Xandra was in no mood for cheerfulness. "Why can't I go back right away? I'll bet I can walk on those things right now." Grabbing the crutches away from Clara, and struggling to stand on her one good leg, she went on, "See? Just watch me." She made a good job of it too, keeping her balance on one leg without too much difficulty and swinging forward on the crutches, but the stubborn man wouldn't say yes. Instead he just laughed and told Clara he was pleased to know at least one student who seemed to hate the thought of missing a single day of school.

Of course Xandra couldn't tell him that it wasn't getting back to school that was so life-and-death important, but that seeing Belinda as soon as possible might be. Seeing Belinda to tell her what had happened in the forest and to ask some questions that had suddenly become much more urgent. So there was nothing more she could say, and the verdict was in. It would be several days, maybe even a week, before she would have a chance to talk to Belinda.

After making another appointment, Clara took Xandra home—but only as far as the lower floor of the house. Xandra very much wanted to go to her own room but Clara said, "I don't think I can carry you the way I used to, darling, so I guess you'll just have to wait until your father or one of your big brothers shows up. I'll just run up and get some of your things and then I'll help you clean up a little in the guest bathroom. Then I'll fix you a place in the family room where you can sit with your leg up and wrapped in an ice pack."

The family room. All day. Xandra hated the idea but at the moment she was just too tired to argue or even complain. "There now, baby." Clara looked worried as she arranged a stack of books and the TV remote on the lamp stand next to Xandra's chair. "I'm going to have to leave now. I have to go to the dentist and then run a few errands. I've left a nice lunch for you in the breakfast room and Geraldine will bring you a fresh ice pack when she comes in. Do you think you'll be all right by yourself for a little while? Otto will be mulching the flower beds all afternoon, and Mildred from the cleaning service is due around one o'clock."

Xandra shrugged and said she didn't need anyone, especially not Mildred, and she'd be *okay*. A grudging okay, which probably made Clara feel even more guilty about going off and leaving her "baby" all alone. Her *ex*-baby, actually. But since she went ahead and left anyway, maybe not quite guilty enough.

So there she was, with a stack of books and the TV remote within easy reach, right in front of the big-screen TV, with nobody else around to decide what they were going to watch. For a few minutes it seemed like an interesting opportunity, but after flipping through the channels, she decided that she just wasn't in the TV mood. The crutches were close by, leaning against the footstool, and around noon Xandra used them for a trip to the breakfast room for lunch, but that was as far as she managed to get.

It was an amazingly long day, with nothing to do but doze off into sleeping nightmares and then wake up to wide-awake ones. To suddenly come back to the daytime world and sit staring into space as she went back over everything that had happened during that horrible night in the forest. Over and over again she brought back what she had done with the Key and how it had allowed the monsters to attack her, except when she was in the white bird's meadow, where the creatures of the Unseen were warm and friendly. The rest of the morning and all afternoon the dreams, sleeping and wide awake, went on and on.

The memory was so sharp and clear that she could feel the itchy tingle where the bites had been, and when she concentrated, she could bring back the soft warmth of those other creatures in the clearing. But what wasn't clear was why any of it had happened and what it meant. How could the feather, which should have been a reward for rescuing the white bird, be the cause of such a horrible experience? And what exactly had Belinda meant when she talked about the Unseen as reflections or mirrors? She knew those were questions only Belinda and the grandfather could answer. And knowing how long it would be before she could even begin to get an answer was terribly frustrating.

After what felt like the longest day of her life, the rest of the Hobsons began to come home from school, and all of them seemed to feel that it was necessary to come in to stare at Xandra and ask all sorts of questions. Of course Gussie came the minute Clara brought her home from kindergarten. Bouncing into the room and dropping an armload of picture books, she was full of questions that tumbled out of her mouth one after the other. Xandra couldn't have answered them all even if she wanted to, which she didn't.

"Xannie," Gussie shrieked, rushing up to throw her arms around Xandra, causing her to lose her place in the book she was reading—or at least pretending to read. "They let you come home. I was afraid you'd be in the hospital for a long time. How is your . . ." And then, seeing the ice pack, "What's that on your leg? Oh, it's cold. Why are they freezing your leg? Does a broken leg feel better when it's frozen?" She noticed the crutches then and grabbed them and stood on tiptoe, trying to make them fit. "Will you have to walk on these now?" And when Xandra nodded, "Oh, you will? Always and forever? Will you have to walk on these forever and ever?"

Xandra had pretty much given up on answering when Clara came in, carrying her purse and a bag of groceries. "Come with me, Augusta," she said. "Don't make a nuisance of yourself. Let Alexandra rest."

"Oh, I'm not being a nuisance," Gussie said, dropping the crutches so that one of them just missed falling on Xandra's wounded leg. "I just want to help Xandra get well. Can't I help you, Xannie? I know what I can do. I can read to you." Grabbing one of her books, Gussie was opening it when Xandra had a better idea. Since Gussie had a reading vocabulary of about a dozen words, a better idea wasn't too hard to come up with.

"I know what you can do for me," Xandra said. "You can go get me something. Okay?"

"Yes, yes. Okay." Gussie was quivering with enthusiasm. "I'll go get you something. What can I get?"

What could Gussie get that might take a long time to find? Xandra thought quickly and came up with "I want one of the animals off my bed. I want . . . I want . . ." (A long pause while she sifted through possibilities, looking for something small and hard to find.) "I know. I want my littlest teddy bear. The little tiny one about as big as this." She held up a forefinger and thumb, thinking that finding that particular bear among forty-six other animals might keep Gussie busy for quite a long time.

Gussie stared big-eyed. "But you said that if I ever touched one of your animals again you'd—"

Glancing at Clara, Xandra interrupted quickly. "Never

mind what I said. I've changed my mind. You just go find that little bear and bring it here. Okay?"

After Gussie charged happily out of the room, Clara asked if there was anything Xandra wanted from the kitchen. "I'm on my way there right now," she said, indicating the bag she was carrying. "A bit of last-minute shopping for Geraldine. She's planning a rather special meal tonight, I think."

"Special?" Xandra asked.

Clara's big smile spread across her face. "In honor of the whole family being able to sit down to dinner at the same time. It's been a while, hasn't it?"

Xandra said she guessed it had been.

Turning to go, Clara stopped long enough to ask, "Or would it be easier for you to have your dinner in your room?"

And without any hesitation Xandra said, "No. I'll eat in the dining room."

Clara left then, and as Xandra watched her go, she was suddenly aware of a fluttering warmth where the feather hung against her chest. Pulling it out, she ran its soft, delicate strength across her hands, closed the fingers of her right hand tightly around it and held it there. But that was all. She did not go on to press it against her forehead. She would not, would never again, use it to enter the world of the Unseen. She would simply keep it, hold on to it and to the memory of what it could do. It was then that she began to notice something, a faint movement at the very edge of her field of vision. Something small and flickering, like a fanning of feathers or a scurry of soft, furry feet. But then the quiver of motion was gone, and although she tried to bring it back, it refused to reappear. She was left alone to think and wonder.

More time—quite a lot of time during which Xandra slept more than she read—passed before Gussie finally returned carrying the teddy bear. Clutching the tiny bear in both hands, she was full of talk about how hard it had been to find. Xandra had been sure it would be. Sure that Gussie would not only have had to dig through forty-seven stuffed animals, but that she also would have had to stop to admire and maybe even to play a little with almost every one of the fascinating creatures that she'd never before been given permission to touch.

Xandra took the bear from Gussie, and after demonstrating how it could be made to stand on its hind feet, she began to make up a story about how she had seen the bear in a store and really liked it but didn't have enough money to buy it. "And when I started to leave," she told a wide-eyed Gussie, "I looked back and saw him running along the counter toward me." She made the little bear run down the arm of her chair. "And when it got to the end of the counter, it jumped down to the floor and dodged around other people's feet trying to catch up with me. I could hear it calling for me to come back. So I grabbed it up before it got stepped on and told the clerk to put it on hold for me. I said, 'Put it in a box with a lid because if you don't, it might run away.' The clerk looked at me like this. . . ." Xandra made a slack-jawed, goggle-eyed expression. "But I made her find a box with a lid. And the next day I went back and there he was. So I gave the clerk the money and brought him home. He's always very happy to see me."

Xandra had never made up a story to tell Gussie before

but she liked the unblinking, openmouthed way the kid listened. When Xandra stopped, she said, "Go on, tell me some more. Tell me some more not-true stories. Not-true stories are my favorite kind."

Xandra was considering another story when some other siblings came in and then quickly went away. This time it was Victoria and then Quincy, who only stayed long enough to learn that the leg wasn't broken before they left, probably to do more important things like playing the piano or feeding fish.

Gussie had gone back upstairs before two more siblings arrived. There they were, both of the Twinsters, in a hurry as usual on their way to change out of their school clothes. Banging through the door, they strutted in, and once again Xandra almost had to agree with the Greek-god thing. To admit that with their bulging football muscles and helmets of curly hair, her Twinster siblings did manage to look a little like Greek gods.

"Hey. So it's not broken after all?" one of them yelled. "So what was all the screaming about, kid?"

Xandra had begun, "Dr. Frank said that sprained ankles hurt worse than—". when the other twin interrupted.

"Hey, how'd you like that stretcher we made out of our jackets? That was pretty cool wasn't it? We learned how to do that last year in first aid class."

"No," the other one said. "That wasn't in first aid. We did that in Boy Scouts a long time ago."

"You're crazy. That wasn't in Scouts. That was Mr. Watson in first aid. Don't you remember how he . . ."

When they left, they were still so busy arguing about where they'd learned to make a jacket stretcher that they forgot to ask Xandra how she was feeling or even to say goodbye.

A few minutes later Clara looked in again on her way upstairs. "Are you sure you feel up to eating in the dining room tonight?" she asked again. "I wouldn't mind bringing you up a tray."

Much to her own surprise, Xandra insisted she could come to the table.

22

AFTER CLARA LEFT the family room, there was still almost half an hour before dinnertime. Half an hour for Xandra to wonder why she'd chosen to eat in the dining room with all the other Hobsons when she could have had a private dinner in her own room, in her own bed, surrounded by her animals. It was a choice that had obviously surprised Clara, not to mention Xandra herself.

It wasn't, she decided, that she was simply postponing facing up to the problem of getting up the stairs, even though there was the embarrassing possibility of having to be carried up by Quincy. Or even worse, by the twins on one of their jacket stretchers. She'd hate that, of course, but she was sure that wasn't the reason for her choice. After all, she was going to have to go upstairs sooner or later, so why not in time for a peaceful dinner in her own room?

Another possibility that she explored and then firmly rejected was that, after a long day pretty much alone in the family room, she was feeling the need to spend some time with other people. That couldn't be it. After all, it had been a long time since she had chosen being with humans, particularly Hobson humans, over being by herself or with animal friends. And that wasn't about to change.

At last she had to conclude that the only real reason for her uncharacteristic decision was that Clara's question had been so sudden and unexpected that she had simply blurted out the first thing that came into her mind.

But unlike herself or not, she had agreed to eat in the dining room, and it was almost time for dinner to begin. It was quite probable that, within a few minutes, someone, or maybe many people, would be showing up to help her get there. Struggling to her one good foot, she grabbed the crutches and hopped and swung her way out of the family room, down the hall and into the dining room so quickly that she was the first one to arrive.

It was an odd feeling. Being the first one to arrive for dinner wasn't a familiar experience for Xandra. In fact, she couldn't remember it ever happening before. Being last had always been much more her style. Last and, more often than not, more than a little late. But there wasn't much point in going out and coming back in again, especially now, when coming and going was so much more complicated than it used to be. So, sighing, she resigned herself to hopping and swinging on down the long table until she came to her usual place. She was in her chair with her crutches propped up on the table beside her, all alone in the huge room, for an unaccustomed and uncomfortable length of time.

For the first few minutes she spent the time looking around the room, at the big marble fireplace directly across from her, and the portrait above it of someone who was supposed to be a more or less famous Hobson ancestor. And then down toward the kitchen door, where other large pictures, landscapes mostly, in gilded frames, hung along the wall. To her surprise, she found it all curiously interesting, almost as if she'd never seen it before, or at least not for a long time. As if, maybe, she'd always been too busy watching people reacting to her late arrival, as well as to the expression on her face, to notice much of anything about the room itself.

She turned then to look behind her at where the long row of floor-to-ceiling windows opened out on the garden. On a garden where the shadows of an early-winter evening were quickly blurring the familiar shapes of shrubs and trees into the gathering darkness. Suddenly she grabbed the edge of the table, staring out into the garden, where a rounded shape that had appeared to be nothing more than a bush now seemed to be moving. The shapeless blob seemed to ooze forward—and then fade into the surrounding shadows.

"Well, look who's here."

Strangely glad to hear a decidedly human voice, Xandra must have been smiling, maybe almost laughing, when she whirled around to see . . . the Twinsters. Both of them looking uncharacteristically uncool, as if they found something startling about Xandra's appearance.

"Hey," one of them said, sounding surprised, amazed even. "You're already here."

Xandra gulped and, still trying to suppress her relieved smile, said, "Yeah, here I am. Where'd you think I'd be at dinnertime?"

With a more typically Twinster expression twisting his lip, one of the twins started to say, "Well, not here. I mean, at least not for another ten or—" He was looking at his watch when the other one whacked him with his elbow.

"Nick just means Clara told us you were in the family room but you weren't so we didn't know where to look." Then Nelson, with a grin slanting toward sarcasm, said, "We were about to get our jackets and head for the forest—" when Nicholas whacked him back.

At that moment there was another interruption as Gussie appeared in the doorway.

"Xannie," Gussie shrieked as she dashed into the room. "There you are. We were looking for you." Skidding to a stop, she almost tripped over Xandra's crutches.

"You were looking for me? You and Clara?"

"No, not Clara. Clara's still changing her dress. *We* were." She pushed the little bear into Xandra's hand. "You went off and left him all alone in the family room and he was scared. He told me he was scared." Leaning closer, she whispered in Xandra's ear, "What's his name?"

"Okay, okay," Xandra whispered back. "His name is Ursa. Ursa Minor but Ursa for short, and you can take care of him." She held the bear up to her mouth, hiding him in the palm of her hand, and pretended to whisper before she gave him back to Gussie. "There. I told him you were going to take care of him. Okay?"

Looking delighted, Gussie ran to her place at the table, dodging around other siblings who were just arriving. Quincy came in first, and then Victoria, and each one of them stared at Xandra, said, "Hi," and then said it again.

She couldn't help noticing that all of the siblings were looking a little bit startled. Some more and some less.

Xandra said, "Hi," and watched each one of their reactions, vaguely wondering why everyone looked so surprised. It did occur to her that they might have been thinking she wouldn't be able to come to the table so soon after her accident. Or else they were just amazed to see her there on time for once? It wasn't until later that it occurred to her to wonder if she had still been smiling. That, she had to admit, might have done it.

Just about then several things began to happen at once. The phone rang and most of the siblings started to jump up, saying, "I'll get it." And "No, it's probably for me. I'm expecting a call." And "No, it's mine. I'm sure of it." But by then it had stopped ringing and people said, "Oh, Clara must have it." And "Yeah, Clara got it." Then they all stared at the door, where Clara would show up in a minute to call somebody to the phone. All but Xandra and Gussie, of course—the only two Hobsons who didn't get many phone calls.

But just as Clara appeared in the doorway, Geraldine stomped in from the other direction, carrying a tray full of bowls and platters.

"Oh dear," Clara said to Geraldine. "That was Mr. Hobson. He said to tell you to put something in the warming oven for him and Mrs. Hobson. They're both going to be late. But he said to go ahead with the children's meal. Here, let me help." Hurrying down the long room, Clara took the tray from a glowering, grumbling Geraldine and they both disappeared into the kitchen.

The Hobson siblings, all of them including Xandra, were left with nothing to do but stare at each other. So they stared and some of them, Victoria for instance, sighed loudly. It was Quincy who broke the silence. "So what else is new?" he said, shrugging and grinning in an angry way.

"Yeah, another big togetherness night at the Hobsons'," one of the twins said sarcastically. And the other twin said, "And another important lesson in family values, in case any of us might forget what's really important around here."

Looking around the table from one face to another, Xandra was feeling puzzled, shocked almost. Shocked to realize that the rest of the siblings felt the same way she did, at least sometimes, and about certain things.

It was one of the twins, Nelson probably, who made a kind of whooping noise. "I got it," he said. "Let's eat really fast and get out of here so when they show up . . ." He spread his hands in an erasing movement. "Nobody. When they show up, we'll be done. Done and . . ." He erased the air again. "*Gone*. Okay, everybody?"

"Okay," the other twin said, and so did Quincy and a moment later Victoria. And then Gussie was asking, "What? What are we going to do? Somebody tell me." Jumping out of her chair, she was racing toward Victoria when Xandra stuck out her arm and stopped her. Pulling Gussie's head down beside her own, she whispered, "We're going to eat very fast and get out of here. Okay?"

"Okay," Gussie said enthusiastically. "Okay." She started back to her chair at her usual dead run and then skidded to a stop. Turning to look back, she whispered, "Why?"

Everybody laughed but it was Xandra who answered first. "For a surprise," she said. And then everyone chimed in.

"Just for fun," one of the twins said.

"It's a new game." That was Victoria.

And then Quincy said, "To give them a taste of their own medicine."

The kitchen door swung open and Clara helped Geraldine pass around platters of lamb chops and bowls of vegetables and potatoes.

"Well," Clara said cheerfully, "what a nice meal. Geraldine, you've given us a banquet as usual." Carrying an empty platter, she once again followed Geraldine into the kitchen before she returned and pulled out her own chair. By the time Clara had lowered herself into her chair, carefully unfolded her napkin and picked up her fork, Geraldine's "banquet" had almost disappeared.

While she shoveled food into her own mouth, Xandra watched Clara's sympathetic smile turn into wonder as, one by one, all the siblings gulped down their last half-chewed mouthful, asked to be excused and left the room.

There was a short traffic jam in the hall when Xandra reached the stairs and resisted being carried up by Quincy. "Why not?" Quincy was asking when the twins butted in, saying they'd get some broomsticks and jackets and be back in a minute.

"No," Xandra wailed. "I want to do it myself."

"But on those crutches?" Victoria asked. "You'll fall."

Xandra was still shaking her head stubbornly when Gussie said, "I know how. Look, Xannie." Sitting down on the bottom stair, Gussie began to push herself backward up to the next step, using her hands and one foot. She made it look easy, and it was. Xandra sat her way to the top of the stairs, got back on the crutches, and a minute later she was once again in her own room.

23

SO THE DAY was finally over and Xandra was back in her room. Back in her own private space with its paintings of enchanted places, and its huge collection of animals. The room she had run out of just the night before, angry beyond thought or reason. But she didn't want to think about that. Not about the forest, or the things that had happened there. At least not so soon. She would sleep first, she decided, and think about it all later, in broad daylight.

Closing the door firmly behind her, she headed directly to her bed with its forty-six animals. (Gussie still had the littlest bear.) Forty-six animals, organized into tidy piles according to size and shape. Obviously Mildred had been in to remake the bed and replace scattered animals since Gussie's visit. The neat stacks were irritating. Neat stacks of animals weren't natural. Sitting on the edge of the bed,

Xandra gently but firmly stirred them up before she collapsed in their midst. But not to sleep. She was much too wide awake.

The problem was she'd slept too much during her long day in the family room. Later, several minutes later, she got back on the awkward crutches and hobbled to the window seat to stare down into the nighttime garden, as she had so often done before. To the garden, where a faint light from the driveway's lamps, sifting in through dangling strands of weeping willow, could turn a scene of manicured lawns and trees into what Xandra had sometimes been able to imagine as an enchanted scene. A scene very like her Garden of Eden painting, where fantastic birds and animals mingled peacefully in an enchanted world.

Leaning forward with her forehead pressed against the windowpane, Xandra squinted and tried to conjure up the familiar scene with its beautiful pairs of lions and leopards and horses and deer. But just when it began to happen, when she was almost able to blend the carefully planned and plotted garden into a beautiful fantasy world, the hard glare of headlights shattered the scene. One of the parents was arriving home. The lights disappeared as Henry's Ferrari curved toward the garages, but only a few minutes later it happened again when the headlights of Helen's Mercedes invaded the garden. So much for the Garden of Eden, Xandra thought, shrugging angrily. The famous Hobson parents had managed to erase the big family dinner, and now they'd done the same to the Garden of Eden. Soon afterward, when Xandra turned back to the window, the sharp edges of lawns and hedges once again began to blur, but changed this time into a shadow-haunted waste-land where the only shapes were vague hollows of darkness.

Feeling suddenly uneasy, Xandra pulled away from the window, blinking and shaking her head. But she didn't leave the window seat, and after rubbing her eyes and taking several deep breaths, she found herself once again leaning forward. And now the changes came more quickly. Vague shapes quickly became horribly familiar hump-backed and hooded forms that oozed in and out of the deepest shadow, now and then pausing to turn eyes like slashes of fire toward her window.

Frozen with fear, Xandra sat as if paralyzed until a knock on the door brought her back to the brightly lit reality of her room—to her bed with its comforting pyramid of animals and to walls lined with bookshelves and plastered with her very personal collection of paintings. Swallowing hard, she managed to call "Come in" before she let her gaze flick quickly back to the window, where the dimly lit garden once more consisted of ordinary plots and plantings. She waited breathlessly as the door swung slowly open, and then she quickly relaxed. It was only Clara.

Only Clara, whose familiar round-faced smile was slanted in a way that Xandra remembered well. The kind of smile that she remembered as meaning something about a shared secret or a joke on somebody. Guessing, Xandra smiled back as she said, "Well, they got home. What did they say?"

"Well, they were surprised, of course," Clara said. A trace of the joking smile was still there. "And maybe a little upset, until I suggested that perhaps you'd all eaten more quickly than usual because . . ." She paused and made the rest of what she had to say into a question. "Because . . . you all needed more time for your homework?"

Xandra did a wide-eyed-innocence bit. "Yeah," she said. "Sure. I'll bet everybody had lots of extra homework tonight."

Before she left, Clara got out Xandra's pajamas and asked if there was anything more she could do, and when Xandra said no there wasn't, Clara offered a hug, which was something else she hadn't done in a long time. And Xandra reacted in a way that had become even more rare and unusual. Not that she hugged back, but neither did she frown and pull away.

Left alone again, Xandra found herself moving slowly and almost against her will back to the window. She was almost there when there was another knock on the door. This time the visitor was Victoria.

Victoria, still in her school clothes and looking . . . well, looking, as always, not exactly glamorous perhaps, but close enough that Xandra couldn't help being reminded of how unfair it was that along with all that musical talent, Tory also got cute and skinny, and the same beautiful teeth as their famous mother.

As Tory walked across the room, her smile had almost, but not quite, the same feeling that it had had back when she and Xandra were much younger, maybe six and eight years old. The difference was—well, there was something in this new smile that recalled the one she'd given the audience before doing her Mozart performance. Wide and bright, but also a little bit nervous, as if she was not sure of her reception. Xandra was wondering about that when

Tory began by saying, "Can you talk about it now? I mean about being lost in the forest all night." She raised her shoulders in a shiver and said it again. "Alone in the forest. All night. I'd have died of fright."

Narrowing her eyes, Xandra checked her female sibling—her sister, that was—for hidden motives. Motives like a plan to tell whatever she learned to the parents, or to gossip about it with the other siblings. Xandra checked carefully and decided she needn't worry. Tory was just curious, maybe even kind of impressed.

So Xandra began, "Well, I guess you heard what the twins and their crummy friends did to me. And it made me so crazy angry—"

"I know. I know," Tory interrupted. "I'd have been furious. But maybe not furious enough to—"

"I didn't plan to do it. I just ran out of the house and on into the forest as hard and as fast as I could. You know how it helps sometimes when you're angry to do something really hard and—"

"Yes. I know. It's like that for me," Tory agreed eagerly. "I've done that sometimes when I was angry. Like running or playing fast, angry music." She smiled then, a little sheepishly. "Or eating. Sometimes when I'm especially angry I just eat a lot, really fast."

Xandra had noticed that. The eating. "Yeah, I know," she said bitterly. "That's one of the things I hate about . . . I mean, I hate it that you can eat like that and still stay so skinny. It just isn't fair."

So then Tory said that Xandra wasn't at all fat, and Xandra said yes, she was, and besides that, "I have these awful crooked teeth and—"

"But you could have had them straightened." Tory looked surprised, amazed almost. "They kept trying to get you to. I heard them. Only you wouldn't. Why wouldn't you?"

"I don't know." Xandra shook her head. She didn't know, not really. "Except it was like they were saying that the way I looked embarrassed them in front of their friends, and so . . ." She shrugged. "So I decided they could just go on being embarrassed, because I didn't have to have straight teeth if I didn't want to."

Tory nodded slowly, looking at Xandra through narrowed eyes. "Okay," she finally said. "I get it. But if you had them done now, and . . ." She stared some more, tipping her head from side to side. "And maybe stopped cutting your hair yourself, you could be really . . ."

Xandra filled the pause with a sarcastic, "Gorgeous. Yeah, sure."

Tory shook her head thoughtfully. "No, not gorgeous."

"How about . . . normal?"

Tory shook her head harder. "No, not just normal. More like . . . beautiful."

Xandra laughed. "Yeah, sure," she said again. And then, "Hey, I thought you wanted to know about what happened last night."

So Xandra went back to her story about being lost all night in the forest. Since she couldn't put in the part about the Unseen, she told mostly about what happened after she got back to the ordinary world and was just sitting on the ground waiting for morning to come. Sitting and waiting, and listening for mountain lions and rattlesnakes. She told it pretty well, throwing in a few extra scary bits like growls and rustling bushes. Well enough, anyway, to make Tory listen without interrupting except for occasionally whispering things like "Oh no," and "I'd have died."

Before she left, Tory, who hadn't been in Xandra's room for quite a while, went around getting reacquainted with Xandra's pictures of enchanted places and making comments about the ones that had always been her favorites, as well as the ones that used to give her nightmares. When the door closed behind Tory, Xandra got back on her crutches and started for the window. Halfway there she turned and went instead to sit in front of the dressing table's mirror to stare at herself. Now and then she pushed back her ragged hair and smiled, imagining hair and teeth like Tory's.

24

I T WAS SEVERAL days before Dr. Frank gave Xandra permission to go back to school, and then only if she went on using the crutches for another week. "At least until next weekend," he said, "and only if someone can drive you to school. Trying to get on and off buses with those crutches might not be a good idea."

That was a big *if* and one that Xandra definitely didn't like. It was absolutely necessary to get back to school and to Belinda as soon as possible. There were too many things that needed answers and explanations. Old answers still needed clarification, and now there was a new and even more urgent question. Why, Xandra needed to ask, were the creatures of the Unseen still there even when they had not been summoned by the Key? Still clearly visible in the dark garden as well as in the house itself.

"I could do the bus thing on crutches. I know I could," Xandra told the doctor. "My parents probably can't pick me up because they're still at work when school gets out and . . . ." But then Clara came to the rescue.

"I think it can be arranged," she said. "I believe Mr. Hobson might be able to drop her off on his way to work, and I am sure I could pick her up." Xandra gave Clara a grateful smile—maybe not a wide, toothy one, but close.

So on Monday morning Xandra finally went back to school, riding in her father's silver Ferarri and arriving only a little bit late. "Well, here you are," the father of the family said as he helped her out of the car, into her backpack and on to her crutches. "Do you need help getting to your class?" he asked, and then looked very relieved when she assured him she could manage. "Very good," he said, glancing at his watch. "I'm due to meet some important people in just a few minutes." He swung himself down into the car, then leaned out the window long enough to call, "Don't forget to wait for Clara. I've arranged for her to be here at three-thirty to pick you up."

Hobbling into Mr. Fernandez's first-period class a little late wasn't quite as bad as she had imagined it would be. Not that she didn't get a lot more attention than usual, but some of it seemed just plain old curiosity, instead of the teasing she'd expected. And there in the second seat in the third row was Belinda, looking the same as always. She was just the same except for how quickly she turned away when Xandra managed to catch her eye. And even more unexpected was how much more difficult it was to find a time for them to talk when no one else was around.

Not that Xandra was concerned about what Marcie

and company, or any of the rest of the class, would do or say if they saw them together. Not anymore. The only thing she really cared about at the moment was getting answers to her questions. But that turned out to be a hard thing to do for more reasons than one. It wasn't just that Belinda didn't seem eager to talk to her, although that was part of it. The main problem was finding a time when the two of them could have even a halfway private conversation.

All that day, every time Xandra tried to talk to Belinda, they were quickly surrounded by other people. People like Katlyn or Melody, or even Marcie herself, who rushed up and butted in to the conversation. Rushed up looking . . . well, it didn't take long to realize that all of them were trying to look more or less like Belinda.

Belinda, it seemed, had become Marcie's latest fad. A fad that included wearing men's suit jackets with rolled-up sleeves instead of coats, and talking in whispers about how much magical power Belinda had, how she was their special friend and how much fun it was to look "different" on purpose. As well as how much their parents hated it. All of which in other circumstances Xandra might have found pretty amusing, but at the moment it meant that every time Xandra started to talk to Belinda, they quickly became a part of the Mob.

It wasn't until the school day was nearly over that Xandra caught sight of Belinda walking by herself on her way to her sixth-period class. Calling, "Hey, Belinda. Wait for me," Xandra hopped and swung as fast as she could on the clumsy crutches, and at last Belinda stopped and waited. But when Xandra finally caught up, Belinda's face was closed, and her cat-at-midnight eyes looked strangely distant and unfocused.

"What is it?" she asked, and then quickly added, "What happened to you?" And then, "You used the Key again, didn't you? After you promised not to."

Xandra nodded guiltily. "Yes, I did. But I didn't mean to. And I wouldn't have except my brothers—two of my siblings and their friends beat up on me and it made me so angry that . . ." She paused then as a bunch of noisy boys crowded past, and when it was quiet enough to talk, she started over in a different place. "Well, anyway, I want to tell you all about it. About everything that happened to me and . . ."

"Yes?" Belinda's eyes were focused now. "You want to tell me everything?"

Xandra nodded hard and rushed on. "But first of all there are some things I just have to find out about. Like, why do I still see them? The Unseen things."

But that was as far as she got before Belinda shook her head and whispered, "No. No, I can't tell you any more. I don't know anything." She was moving away when Xandra grabbed her arm and held on.

"Yes, you do. You and your grandfather. He knows about all sorts of supernatural stuff, doesn't he? He could tell me all about it if he wanted to. Couldn't he?"

When Belinda turned back, her face was tense, tight-mouthed and narrow-eyed. "Hush," she said. "Don't talk about my grandfather. Don't you say anything about him. Do you hear me?" Then she turned away and, walking so fast Xandra had no chance to catch up, disappeared into a passing crowd of students.

Left alone in the hall, Xandra stared after Belinda before she swung around clumsily and clumped back to her class.

She didn't see Belinda again, even though she watched for her in the hall and later out in front of the school while she waited for Clara to arrive. She was facing away from the street, checking every group of kids as they poured out down the steps to the sidewalk, when suddenly something grabbed her arm, almost making her lose her balance. It was Gussie.

"Hi," Gussie shrieked. "Hi, Xandra. Clara and me came to pick you up."

"Well, take it easy," Xandra said. "You almost knocked me over." She looked around. "Where is she? I don't see her car."

"I'm sorry," Gussie said, bouncing up and down on her toes the way she always did when she was excited. "I didn't mean to bump you. Clara's way down there." She pointed to the end of a line of waiting cars. "She came to get you and she let me come too. I wanted to help you. I wanted to help carry your books. May I? Please may I carry your books?"

So Xandra had to stop and balance on one leg while she got out of her backpack before they could get started down the sidewalk to Clara's car. Once there, Gussie went on making a nuisance of herself. After holding Xandra's crutches while she got in, Gussie shoved them into the car with so much enthusiasm she whacked Xandra on the leg, and then she dropped the backpack into the gutter while she was trying to put it on the seat. When they were both safely inside, Xandra breathed a sigh of relief.

As Clara pulled away from the curb, Xandra turned to the window, still checking for Belinda, but mostly looking away from Gussie. Looking away but still very much aware of Gussie's big eyes and eager baby-toothed smile and also aware of the high-pitched kid-on-television voice that kept asking questions like "How is your broken leg, Xandra? Does it hurt? Does it hurt all the way up or just down there where the bandage is?"

At last Xandra turned back toward Gussie, sighed again, and said, "It's okay. It doesn't hurt at all anymore. Mostly it just itches under the bandage."

"Itches?" Gussie started to unfasten her seat belt. "I could scratch it for you. I'm a good scratcher."

"No. No. Not now. Fasten your seat belt."

Clara yelled the same thing. "Fasten your seat belt, Gussie. Right now!"

Gussie did. Looking startled and then dramatically tragic, she struggled to get the clip to snap and went on struggling until Xandra reached over and did it for her. When it was done, she looked up at Xandra through her insanely long eyelashes and did a quivery smile, and without planning to, Xandra reached over and gave her a hug.

That night after dinner Xandra went to her room early, very tired from clumping around on crutches all day. Tired or not, she went directly to the window, but although she waited and watched for several minutes, the garden was its old self, neatly dull and uninteresting. Getting into her pajamas, she threw herself down on her bed and was just lying there among all her animals when something began to happen. She smelled it first, that same old interesting slightly skunky odor, and then a whiff of the soft milky smell of a very young kitten. There were sounds too, a soft, quickly fading purr, and a distant clatter that might have been the beginning of a baby barn owl's call. Sitting up quickly, she looked around the room, but there was nothing to see. Only the packed full bookshelves and above them the pictures and posters. It wasn't until she squinted and glanced quickly from side to side that she saw, or almost saw, something small and fuzzy skittering along the baseboards and disappearing from sight around the open closet door. That was all, but it was enough to remind her of what she had been told about the Unseen. That they were everywhere, all the time.

Very soon afterward she went to sleep and woke up feeling, well, not great, perhaps, but a lot better than sometimes. By getting out of bed immediately she managed to be the first one, the first sibling at least, at breakfast. Only Helen, the lawyer/mother, was there, having her coffee while she leafed through a stack of papers. When Xandra came in, she marked her place carefully before she said. "Well, hello, dear. What a surprise." And some other things about how pleased she was about Xandra's "very real" recent improvements like being places on time. "And," she said, smiling and raising her famous eyebrows, "no more intrafamily altercations, at least none that I've been privy to."

Xandra didn't appreciate the stuff about "very real improvements," as if she'd only made phony ones before, but she didn't let it spoil her good mood. Instead she even dropped a hint or two about how she might have changed her mind about having her teeth straightened. And later on the way to school she brought up the subject with the father, who said it was fine with him and he'd ask Clara to arrange it right away.

But school was a terrible letdown. Belinda wasn't there. At home sick, maybe, Xandra thought. Lots of people had been out that month with some kind of stomach flu. The kind that hit hard but usually didn't last very long. Most people were only out for two or three days, but on Friday Belinda still wasn't there. It was Friday afternoon that Xandra went to talk to the school secretary and found out that it wasn't the flu at all. It was a lot worse.

"Oh no," Mrs. Green, the secretary, said. "Belinda is leaving. She came in yesterday morning to ask how to go about getting her records sent to another school."

"Another school? What school?" Xandra was dismayed. "Where is she going?"

"She didn't say." Mrs. Green seemed to be very busy. As she started to pick up the phone, she said, "Perhaps she'll let you know." While Xandra was still standing there staring, Mrs. Green dialed a number and began to talk. Xandra went out to meet Clara and Gussie in a state of shock. She was quiet on the way home and Gussie, for once in her life, was quiet too, as if she understood.

But it was that night at dinner that another "intrafamily altercation" happened and this time it definitely wasn't Xandra's fault. At least it didn't start out that way. Henry, the stockbroker, was home in time for dinner that night but not Helen, the lawyer. But right there at the dinner table in front of everybody, Henry started asking Clara to call Dr. Baldwin, the family orthodontist, to arrange some appointments for Alexandra. Xandra cringed, expecting the worst, and it happened. One of the twins grinned at her and said something sarcastic about how a certain party must have changed her mind about refusing to run for Miss America. Not everyone at the table heard him, but the ones who did, the other twin and Quincy, had been a part of an old argument about Miss America contests. An argument in which Xandra always said beauty contests were stupid and insulting and the rest of them usually made remarks about how she was just jealous of good-looking girls.

The other twin and Quincy laughed and said things like "As if," and "Good luck, kid, you'll need it." And then all three of them just sat there grinning at her until she jumped up, picked up her glass and threw the water at the nearest twin, who happened to be the one who had started it. And then, forgetting all about her crutches, she ran out of the room and up the stairs.

It wasn't until later that she remembered about the crutches and decided it didn't matter. She was supposed to quit using them tomorrow anyway. And if her ankle had hurt at all on her way up the stairs, she'd been too angry to notice it.

Back on the window seat in her own room, it wasn't her leg that was hurting. But a hurting was there, all right, so strong and fierce that she could smell it. A smoky smell she remembered well, bitter and biting in her nose and throat. Before she even turned to the window and looked down, she knew she would see them, and she did, oozing out of the darkest shadows and glancing up at her with fiery eyes. Shuddering, she turned quickly away and got ready for bed.

She was hiding under the covers and armloads of animals, but still very much aware of frightening smells and sounds, when she suddenly heard something quite different. The loud, only too real rattle of a doorknob, and a familiar voice whispering her name. Sitting up, she looked toward the door in time to see something sliding under it. Something small and white and flat.

The note said, "Hey, I'm sorry. Anyway I didn't mean it the way you took it. You'd be a red-hot Miss America candidate. And when you get crowned, instead of crying, you could say you think the whole thing is stupid."

It was signed "Nicholas" and there were two PS's. The first one said, "Good shot with the water. Got me right in the eye." And the second one, in print, said, "Yeah. Good shot. And he deserved it." It was signed "Nelson."

The note was still in her hand when she went to sleep, and when she woke up a few hours later, sniffing cautiously before she sat up, the only smells were of clean sheets, furniture polish and dusty stuffed animals. However, she couldn't get back to sleep right away, and before she did, she'd made up her mind. On Saturday she would go back to the commune to look for Belinda.

25

IT WAS A dark, sunless day. The bus ride was long and slow and would have been boring if Xandra hadn't had worse things than boredom to worry about. Things like whether she would get to the commune only to find that Belinda and the grandfather were already gone. And if they were still there, how they would react to her uninvited visit? What was the first thing she should say to them, and what might their answers be? She had plenty of time to go over all of it again and again before the bus finally pulled up to the lonely bus stop where Belinda had been waiting for her when she came before. But today no one was waiting, and no one else got off the bus at the run-down service station. In fact, Xandra had a distinct feeling that the other people on the bus were all staring at her as she rang the buzzer and then went down the steps, as if they couldn't imagine why anyone would want to get off at a place like that.

She didn't blame them. If she'd still been sitting in the warm, well-lit bus, she'd probably have been feeling the same way. As the bus pulled away, she couldn't help staring after it enviously for a minute before she started to look around. To look first at the shabby service station and then up the lonely dirt road that led to Ezra's farm and the deserted commune.

The sky was gray and getting grayer. No rain as yet, but lots of low-hanging clouds and not a hint of sunlight anywhere. Under the dull, heavy sky the service station looked as lonely and forsaken as a scene from a science fiction movie about a world where everyone had died many years before. However, when Xandra looked more closely, she noticed a bit of light coming through the dirty windows, so someone might be in there after all. Remembering what Belinda had said about using the service station's pay phone, Xandra was suddenly overtaken by an urge to do exactly that. To go into the station and use the phone to call a taxi to take her back home. For a few moments she seriously considered it, but then she squared her shoulders, took a deep breath and started off up the dirt road.

The car dump came first. A place where people must have been dumping the crumpled and rusted bodies of their very dead cars for a great many years. Soon after the car dump was the first of three small tumbledown houses. And then nothing more for a long way except weed-grown fields. Just as before, all that empty space gave Xandra an uneasy, no-place-to-hide feeling, which she tried to ignore without much success. Turning up the collar of her coat against the bitter cold, she went on walking determinedly, one foot before the other, until she came at last to the driveway that led up the hill to Ezra's farmhouse.

After dragging open the heavy gate, Xandra made her way up the driveway that led to the shabby old farmhouse. With its dangling shutters and rust-stained walls, it needed only a bat or two to look exactly like an advertisement for Halloween. With her mind flitting between haunted houses and Ezra's angry stare, Xandra walked as quietly and as fast as possible. She finally arrived at the crest of the hill, from which it was possible to look down into the deserted valley where one hundred people had once lived in a commune called Ezra's Eden. A few steps farther on she was able to see the larger of the rough, unpainted shacks, and then the one that had been Belinda's special living space.

There was no sign of life in either cabin. No light in the windows and no smoke rising from the chimney of the larger one, as there had been when she was there before. Xandra stopped and stared, hesitant to go any farther and yet determined to be absolutely certain they were gone before she gave up and went away. She continued on down the hill slowly and watchfully. On reaching Belinda's cabin, she again hesitated before she climbed the rickety stairs, almost sure that she would find the interior completely empty and deserted. But maybe not. Maybe not yet. Hastily, she opened the door and stepped inside.

Just as she had feared, the main room of the cabin was bare. Or almost bare. The rough wooden walls no longer held Belinda's collection of pictures and posters, and there were no books on the rough plank shelves. But sitting near the empty shelves there was a row of small sturdy boxes. Moving from box to box, Xandra confirmed her suspicion. The boxes were full of neatly packed books. So there was still hope. Belinda would never go away and leave her books, which probably meant that she and the grandfather were still around and might be back very soon. And when they arrived . . .

Sitting down on one of the biggest boxes, Xandra prepared herself to wait. But she had not been waiting long when all sorts of worrisome possibilities came to mind. What if they had already gone away and were planning to send for the books at some later time, perhaps days later? And even worse, much worse, what if they had been preparing to leave when something happened to them? Perhaps something terrible. Something like . . .

Xandra was at about that point in her thinking when the shaky shack reverberated to the sound of running footsteps on the stairs and the door flew open—on Belinda.

Xandra jumped to her feet. "Oh, Belinda," she said, and for just a moment Belinda's face echoed her happy surprise, before it closed into a tight, suspicious mask. "What are you doing here?" she whispered.

"You're leaving?" Xandra's answering whisper was both a question and an accusation. "They told me at the school that you were leaving and I just had to see you again before—"

"Why? Why did you have to see me? Haven't you caused us enough trouble?"

"Me? Caused who trouble?"

"Me and my grandfather."

"Caused you and your grandfather trouble? How did I

do that?" she asked, although she was beginning to get the feeling that maybe she knew. "You mean by telling those girls that you had magical powers? What was wrong with that? They deserved to be scared a little. And I thought you must have liked the way it changed things. I mean, it sure did change how those girls were treating you. I thought that was why you wouldn't talk to me anymore, because you had so many new friends you didn't need me anymore."

"No." Belinda was shaking her head. "No, I didn't like it. I tried to stop them but I couldn't and then someone told her parents and the parents called the school and . . ." She paused and then went on. "And that's why we're leaving."

Xandra was amazed. "I don't understand," she said. "Why would that make you leave?"

"Because it happened before. Where we used to live someone started telling people my grandfather was an evil person. And there were some people there, where we used to live, who believed in evil powers and things like that." Belinda's deep eyes focused sharply on Xandra's face. "But he isn't evil. He never does anything to hurt people. He's just a special kind of thinker who sees in a different way and knows about things other people haven't learned about. But some people thought he was dangerous and that was why we had to come here to live."

Still bewildered, Xandra said, "But I thought you liked it here, in the commune."

"Like it?" Looking around, Belinda shrugged and threw out her hands dismissively. "Do I like this dirty old place?" She looked pained and sad.

For a moment the word "dirty," as in "a place with no vacuum cleaner," made Xandra wince. It was a guilty wince but she shook off the guilt and said, "But I don't see how it could be my fault. I didn't mean to get you into trouble." Xandra was still insisting when another voice answered, "No, I'm sure you didn't." Xandra whirled around to see a tall, narrow figure in the open doorway. The grandfather.

Startled and fearful, Xandra was backing away when the man's dark eyes met hers and she stood still, steadied and no longer frightened. "You meant no harm," he was saying, "and Belinda was also speaking truthfully when she said we meant you no harm. And yet I'm afraid I did harm you by letting Belinda show you how to use your Key to evoke the world of the Unseen. I should have met you first and learned more about who you were. If I had, I would have understood that it was . . . too soon."

"Too soon for what? If it was too soon, why did I get the feather? The Key, that is."

The grandfather shook his head. "It's hard to say exactly why, except that merely having it in your possession might only have made you *aware* of the world of the Unseen, instead of being a part of it. And that awareness might have made it possible for you to—"

"Aware of?" Xandra interrupted. "You mean I would have seen those things sometimes but they wouldn't have been able to hurt me?"

"Yes, exactly."

Xandra stared from the grandfather to Belinda and back again before she burst out, "But what are they? Where do they come from and what are they?"

The grandfather nodded slowly before he began. "They

191

are everything and nothing," he said. "A flowing river of shapeless elements that take on definite shapes only when they enter a person's field of energy. And even then they ordinarily cannot be experienced by the sense organs of humans without the use of a Key. Do you understand what I'm saying?"

Xandra nodded uncertainly at first and then more confidently. "I think so."

"Yes, I think you do," the grandfather said. "Although such forms are entirely invisible to ordinary eyes and ears, the shapes they take on seem to be influenced by, or reflections of, each individual's feelings and emotions. But if a person has never possessed a Key, she only experiences them as a kind of inner awareness." He paused and smiled before he went on, "As when an angry person says, 'It was really eating at me,' or, 'I am burning up.' Or as another person might say that something was giving them 'good vibes' or 'a great feeling.' But the use of a Key takes one into their world. The world of the Unseen."

"But I can still see them sometimes," Xandra said. "Even when I haven't used the Key."

"And you will continue to, I think," the grandfather said. "Even when you no longer have the Key."

Xandra narrowed her eyes as she shoved her hand between the buttons of her coat to where she could feel the living warmth of the white bird's gift. "When I no longer have . . ." she was beginning to ask when Belinda grabbed her arm.

Pushing her toward the door, Belinda said, "Come on. We have to go now and so do you. I'll walk with you as far as the gate."

They didn't talk much on their way up the hill. With her mind sifting through a whirling mass of ideas and feelings, Xandra said nothing at all until they had passed the crest of the hill and were on their way across the farmyard. It was then that she asked, "What did he mean when he said when I no longer have the Key?"

Belinda nodded and answered, "He told you before. No one has one for long."

Xandra thought of protesting, of saying she would never, ever, for any reason give up her enchanted gift, but when she turned to Belinda and began to speak, she found she'd lost her train of thought. Instead she asked, "Will I see you again? Will you let me know where you are and how we can go on being friends?"

Without hesitating Belinda said, "Yes, I will."

And Xandra knew that it was true.

26

WHEN CLARA, WHO as usual was the only one to notice that Xandra had been gone most of Saturday, asked where she had been, Xandra quickly thought up a reasonable-sounding excuse. It wasn't until after she'd said it that she realized it was the truth, or at least a part of the truth. What she said was "My best friend is moving away and I went to tell her goodbye."

And when Clara said, "I see. But I do wish you'd tell me when you go out," Xandra stared at her soft round face and worried eyes and said, "Maybe I will, next time. Yeah, I promise. Next time I will."

Later that night, when she was in bed trying to read, but mostly thinking about what the grandfather had said, there was a soft knock on the door. A light, uncertain tapping before the door opened just a crack. Dropping her book and scattering a layer of animals, Xandra sat up quickly and, just as quickly, relaxed. The eye that was peeking through the crack was at a level that suggested either a smallish creature of the Unseen—or possibly . . .

"All right, Gussie, I see you," Xandra said. "Come on in."

The door swung wide and Gussie bounced across the room to launch herself, facedown, into the middle of Xandra's animal collection. Pushing to a sitting position, she started checking out the nearest animals, which happened to be a pig, an alligator and a shaggy Chincoteague-type pony. As Gussie hugged, kissed and whispered to each toy, Xandra watched with curiosity. Gussie was acting, Xandra decided, like a kid who'd never played with a stuffed animal toy before, which certainly wasn't the case.

"Hey, kid," Xandra said. "What's the big deal? Your room is full of stuffed animals."

Clutching the pony to her chest, Gussie nodded enthusiastically. "I know," she said. "But yours are better."

"How come?"

Gussie thought for a moment, tipped her head, smiled her killer smile and said, "Because they're yours."

Xandra was still thinking that one over when Gussie reached into her pocket, brought out the tiny teddy bear and said, "I had to bring Ursa back."

And when Xandra said, "No, you didn't. I gave him to you, remember?" Gussie nodded and said, "I know. But he was lonely for all his old friends, especially the bears. He's really lonesome for the bears."

So Xandra let Gussie crawl around the bed for a while

reintroducing Ursa Minor to all the other bears before she said, "Okay, kid. Enough is enough." Shoving a very large shaggy bear into Gussie's hands, she said, "Here, take Baloo with you. He'll keep Ursa company."

That night when the lights were off, Xandra worked at the awareness thing, listening and sniffing, squinting and doing quick sideways glances. But there was nothing—at least nothing for sure. Once or twice there was a brief purring sound, and one other time a fleeting smell of newborn kitten. But that was all. And nothing at all that hinted at hooded figures with fiery eyes and flashing teeth.

But the very next evening there was another "intra-family altercation" of a sort. It happened in the family room, over what channel they were going to watch. The twins weren't there, so the participants were Victoria and Xandra on one side and Quincy on the other. Quincy only won because he was bigger and stronger, which was especially unfair because Quincy could have gone to his own room and watched it on his own "overprivileged-eighteen-year-old's" private TV. Except that he kept saying it was the kind of movie that needed to be seen on a giant screen. So he sat there and watched the stupid wide-screen war movie while Xandra got more and more infuriated. Some yelling had gone on, most of it by Xandra, before Tory suggested that she and Xandra go to her room and play Scrabble, which they did.

That was something they hadn't done for a long time, so all by itself, that was a big change. And another change was that Xandra didn't get upset when Tory won two out of their three games. At least not very. But later that night, when Xandra was sitting on the window seat, she thought she saw a dark hooded figure oozing between tree trunks and hedges. Just about then, however, an owl flew by and while Xandra watched its flight, the hooded shadows blended into the smooth and silent night.

The next week went by like that, with only vague hints of Unseen creatures, and then one morning when Xandra woke up, the Key was gone. The strong necklace of heavy string was still around her neck but the feather had disappeared. It had been there the night before and there was no way it could have been taken without her knowing. She searched everywhere, under and around every stuffed animal, under the bed and between the blankets, before she allowed herself to remember that she'd been warned that it would happen.

Even while she was remembering that both Belinda and the grandfather had told her that no one had a Key for long, Xandra felt miserable and angry. And she started the day by letting everyone know it, without, of course, telling them why. She was still feeling angry and ill-treated when she got off the school bus that afternoon, and there they were, both of the Twinsters, waiting for her in the driveway of the Hobson Habitat. She was suspicious at first, with good reason. And then very much surprised.

One of the twins, Nelson she thought at first, but it turned out to be Nicholas, was holding a large cardboard box and in the box were three very young kittens.

"Hey," Nicholas said. "Look what we brought you. Three new candidates for the Xandra Hobson Society for the Prevention of Kitten Murder."

"Yeah," Nelson said. "These guys we know were about to throw these dudes in the river when we came to the rescue." He grabbed the box out of Nicholas's hands. "Come on. Let's take them down to the basement."

Xandra was so surprised she almost forgot to be angry. But on the way to the basement she demanded to know how they knew. "When did you find out about . . . about what I do in the basement?"

They both laughed. "We've known for years," Nicholas said, and Nelson added, "We've always known. We used to check it out every once in a while when you weren't around. The owl was pretty cool."

"And the skunk." Nicholas was laughing. Holding his nose, he said, "That skunk was really breathtaking."

"You knew? But you didn't tell on me?"

Nelson grinned and shrugged. "We figured it was your business."

So Xandra was busy in the basement again, and this time the twins were in on it too. Like buying kitten milk at the pet store and asking their friends about people who might want to adopt a kitten in the near future. Of course they could still be disgusting, like when they started calling Xandra M.M., which stood for Metal-Mouth because of the braces on her teeth. And by just naturally being their cocky, teenage Greek-god selves.

And as for Belinda? Xandra thought about her every day, remembering all the secret private things they had been able to talk about. But she also remembered Belinda's promise that they would meet again, and how she, Xandra, had known immediately that it was true.

In the meantime Christmas came and went, and there

were still nights on the window seat when Xandra thought she saw fiery eyes in the dark garden. But then more often than not a silent owl-shaped shadow would drift by, and when she opened the window she would detect a faint aroma of baby skunk.